Praise for *Not Before Sundown* (a.k.a ...

'Blame global warming, but trolls are moving out of legend to scavenge at the outskirts of Finnish cities . . . Sinisalo's strange and erotic tale peers at the crooked world through a peephole. The troll comes to life after hours, unleashing glittering desires . . . Is the troll becoming more human (hurt, jealousy), or does he merely reveal our own trollishness?' – *Guardian*

'Unsettlingly seductive . . . elegance, authenticity and chilling conviction'
– *Independent on Sunday*

'Chillingly seductive' – *Ind*

'A sharp, resonant, prickly
and gay fiction.' – Neil G

'An imaginative and enga[g]
voices nicely underscore the moral of Sinisalo's ingeniously constructed fable:
The stuff of ancient legend shadows with rather unnerving precision the course
of unloosed postmodern desire.' – *Washington Post*

'Simple but very powerful . . . A thoughtful, inspiring and rewarding work.'
– *Gay Times*

'A wily thriller-fantas[
reminding us of how

'A punk version of *T*[
myths while ditching
book exploits the co[
them . . . This smart,
[and] underscores h[
– *USA Today*

'A brilliant and dark
animal . . . Johanna S[
later you're holding y[
granted.' – *The Boston*

'Sinisalo takes us on a brilliant and sometimes horrifying multidisciplinary adventure through biology and belief, ecology, morality, myth and metaphysics, in a quest for a wild place where trolls can run free.' — *Creative Loafing*

'Sinisalo uses the relationship between man and troll to examine the hidden motivations in human–human interactions . . . Sinisalo sets up thematic connections between nearly every event in the book, but she handles them with a light touch . . . this would be Ibsen's *The Wild Duck* — if the duck were the main love interest. Granted, Ibsen's doomed waterfowl never ended up in a pair of designer jeans, but both creatures highlight the uneasy role of feral nature trapped within civilized humanity.' — *Village Voice*

'While trolls in legends and stories often resemble werewolves, changelings and demons, in Sinisalo's book it's the humans whose beastly qualities are familiar and threatening. Her in-translation language is marvelous, sexy, enticing . . . Blood and bone mixes with unique humor and wit.' — *San Diego Union Tribune*

'Johanna Sinisalo has created a strange, beautiful tale, expertly translated, and cinematic enough for movie scenes . . . Thought-provoking, uniquely imaginative, and brimming with circus-sideshow details. . . Sinisalo's story ascends to more than just a freakish attraction by being intellectual and darkly comic all at once. The result is simply brilliant.' — *San Francisco Bay Reporter*

'Told as a modern-day fairy tale . . . it haunted me long after I finished. It has all the elements, including some of the disturbing ones, found in so many of Grimm's stories, but is nonetheless a truly original novel.' — *Powells.com*

'Offers an ingenious dramatization of the nightmare of blurred boundaries between species and a disturbing dystopian vision reminiscent of Karel Capek's classic *War with the Newts*. A fascinating black comedy, from a writer who has made the transition to literary fiction with a giant's stride.' — *Kirkus Reviews* (starred review)

'A sexually charged contemporary folk tale . . . Sinisalo's elastic prose is at once lyrical and matter-of-fact . . . The troll brings out Angel's animal instincts, representing all the seduction and violence of the natural world.' — *Publishers Weekly*

'The comedy is irresistible, the pages turn themselves, carried along by the quicksilver of an unbelievably imaginative pen . . . Run to this book . . . An entertaining variation on the eternal confrontation between man and beast, the light and dark angels that live in all of us.' — *Télérama* (Paris)

JOHANNA SINISALO was born in Finnish Lapland in 1958. She studied theatre and drama and worked in advertising for a number of years before becoming a full-time author, at first writing science fiction and fantasy short stories. Her acclaimed first novel *Not Before Sundown* (2000) – also published by Peter Owen – won the prestigious Finlandia Award and the James Tiptree Jr Award for works of science fiction or fantasy that expand or explore our understanding of gender. Also known in Finland for her television and comic-strip writing, she has won the Atorox Prize for best Finnish science fiction or fantasy story seven times and has been the winner of the Kemi National Comic Strip Contest twice. In addition to her four novels she has written reviews, articles, comic strips, film and television scripts and edited anthologies, including *The Dedalus Book of Finnish Fantasy*. Her short story 'Baby Doll' was a Nebula nominee and Grand Prix de l'Imaginaire nominee in France, and it was published in the *Year's Best SF 13* anthology in the USA. Her work has been translated into twenty languages, including twelve translations of *Not Before Sundown*.

BIRDBRAIN

Also by Johanna Sinisalo and published by Peter Owen

NOT BEFORE SUNDOWN

BIRDBRAIN

Johanna Sinisalo

Translated from the Finnish
by David Hackston

PETER OWEN
London and Chicago

PETER OWEN PUBLISHERS
73 Kenway Road, London SW5 0RE

English language edition first published in Great Britain 2010
by Peter Owen Publishers

Translated from the Finnish *Linnunaivot*
© Johanna Sinisalo 2008

English translation © David Hackston 2010

Cover artwork Hannu Mänttäri

ISBN 978-0-7206-1343-8

A catalogue record for this book is available from the British Library

Printed in the UK by CPI Bookmarque Ltd, Croydon, CR0 4TD

This project has been funded with support from the European Commission. This
publication reflects the views only of the author, and the Commission cannot be held
responsible for any use which may be made of the information contained therein.

Education and Culture DG
Culture Programme

'Be that word our sign of parting, bird or fiend!' I shrieked, upstarting –
'Get thee back into the tempest and the Night's Plutonian shore!
Leave no black plume as a token of that lie thy soul hath spoken!
Leave my loneliness unbroken! – quit the bust above my door!
Take thy beak from out my heart, and take thy form from off my door!'
    Quoth the raven, 'Nevermore.'

– Edgar Allen Poe, *The Raven* (1845)

SOUTH COAST TRACK, TASMANIA
Cockle Creek to South Cape Rivulet
Monday, March 2007

HEIDI

Hanging around a modest distance from the Tassielink minibus terminus is a group of guys, their shorts boasting rips and tears, their T-shirts with stains, their armpits and backs with patches of sweat, their hiking boots with layers of dried mud. Jyrki gets out of the bus first, looks around, his brow furrowed, but as soon as he sees the row of trekkers his face brightens. He raises his hand in a gesture of calculated nonchalance, as if to say 'Hi, we're cut from the same cloth', and the group manages a few mumbled greetings.

They're standing in the shade at the edge of the dust track, a group of six young men, their bags a collection of bundles and straps, their beards scruffy and unkempt, as I step out into the sunshine and stretch my arms and legs. The drive from Hobart has taken over three hours. We're the only passengers to travel all the way to the end of the line. The driver lifts the tarpaulin covering the trailer and dumps our rucksacks on the dusty verge.

The midday sky is like a bright-blue dome. Cockle Creek is full of gentle grassy slopes, tidy bushes, footbridges across narrow, sandy channels of sea, families enjoying a picnic. Toddlers squealing with excitement and fear of the cool water are splashing about in the wash with their brightly coloured floats. My eyes automatically start scanning around for a café, a restaurant, an ice-cream stand, a souvenir shop. The only sign of civilization is an outdoor toilet cubicle hidden in the thicket.

I can't help wondering what it must be like to be one of those grime-covered guys, the smell of sweat lingering in the air metres around them, to arrive here from South Coast Track only to discover that you've missed the only minibus of the day by a few minutes. From Cockle Creek it must be a good thirty kilometres to the nearest place offering any kind of facilities. You'll have to wait a day for the next bus, sometimes two days, enjoying the pleasures of the non-existent local infrastructure. There is no through-traffic here, so even hitch-hiking would be limited to the cars of the families out on a day trip.

Still, I know exactly what Jyrki would say in a situation like that. We'll walk, he'd say.

JYRKI

OK, now you can open your eyes. Three guesses where we are.

Beep! Wrong answer.

This was supposed to be the edge of the Southwest National Park. This was supposed to be almost in the Great Outback.

Correct answer: this is a nothing but a spruced-up, sanitized, middle-class playground.

Take that campsite over there, the one we just passed. Enormous caravans parked on the grassy parkland; giant awnings with multiple rooms and plastic windows hoisted up alongside them, tents bigger that your average downtown flat, crammed full of functional furniture fashioned in the best traditions of cheap plastic design. Wheezing outdoor barbeques, guzzling gas from cylinders, turning the air glassy and shimmering. On the camping table the antennae of a travel television points up towards the sky like a victory sign.

These people leave their concrete suburban hell behind them, billowing litre upon litre of petrol into the atmosphere in the process, and for a brief moment set up a plastic hell here at the edge of the bush. All this so that they can tell their friends about how great it was roughing it for a couple of nights – standing there taking their GM-soya-fattened pork chops out of their polystyrene packaging and throwing them on the barbie to sizzle; fetching a six-pack of Fosters from the Winnebago fridge, chilled by keeping the car's engine idling all day. It's wild out there and oh so liberating. A real tale of survival.

If we put up our Hilleberg tent out here, it would look like a kennel on Millionaires' Row. Someone might accidentally step on it, crush it like an ant.

At Overland Track the scent of untouched nature was much more distinct. Although there was a large guide centre, a café and even a hotel at the start of the track, everything about the place said that you only needed to walk a hundred metres and the sense of being in the outback would whistle in your ears like a bone flute.

The driver, a friendly man with a freckled bald patch, is already lugging the returning hikers' rucksacks into the trailer at the back of the minibus. I exchange a few words with our fellow trekkers. The words 'mud' and 'Ironbound' come up again and again. The weather has apparently been all right.

It's rained a bit, but there's been no flooding. At Cox Bight a wombat had spent all evening grazing right next to the campsite.

The guys' chilled-out, relaxed, indirect way of bragging is an unspoken indication that we're not quite in the same league. Picking up on their carefully suppressed blokish chest-beating makes the bottom of my stomach tingle, that same sense of expectation as when I was younger, going out on the pull after an evening shift. Without saying a word, the group's body language makes it clear that they had served their time while we were just arriving at the barracks.

She's standing next to me, listening solemnly to our colleagues' stories. They've reached that ecstatic phase, raving on about the first things they want once they reach Hobart: a cold beer, a hot shower, a bed with crisp linen and fresh food seem to be at the top of everyone's list.

I tell them that in Finland the first thing men coming back from the front wanted was sex; only after that did they take their skis off. The lads give an uncertain chuckle.

I hoick my rucksack from the sand and up over my shoulder. You have to do this quickly, without any obvious effort, without catching your breath.

The driver says his compulsory farewells and wishes us luck. The doors of the minibus slam shut.

In a cloud of dust and exhaust fumes, our umbilical cord is severed.

I ask her if we're ready. She nods, almost imperceptibly.

At the start of the track there is a wooden shelter with three walls featuring laminated guides to the national park and a couple of information notices. Also, on a small shelf, there is a registration book with a pen on the end of a piece of string.

She flicks through the book and asks whether we ought to write our names down.

Standing there, holding that book, she's holding on to Cockle Creek with both hands, delaying our departure like a small child on her way to the dentist. When you leave something difficult alone, avoid it and procrastinate long enough, eventually it will go away.

HEIDI

I hesitate, shifting my weight from one foot to the other, because I want the group of three energetic-looking guys that arrived shortly after us in a car to go first so they'll get enough of a head start on us. Then I might be spared the inevitable embarrassment of people trekking behind us first overtaking us, then hanging around taking photographs or stopping for a piss, then, before you know it, breathing down your neck again. Excuse me, but would the lady mind letting us past? It's obvious they'll be faster than us – faster than *me*, that is. We'll meet them in South Cape Bay later that evening anyway – and why shouldn't we meet them? It's already half past twelve, and I doubt even a herd of testosterone-fuelled bulls like them could make it any further by nightfall.

Jyrki comes and stands beside me, rests a heavy, purposeful arm on my shoulder and looks around. In the battered old ring-binder someone has taken a ruler and a biro and drawn columns where people fill in their names, the date and an estimate of how long they think they're going to be out on the trail.

Shattering the whiteness of the registration book and drawing a pen across the paper feels almost like taking an oath, a deed that would have repercussions far beyond the act of simply writing down my name.

But isn't it precisely those kind of deeds I've come here to take on?

Jyrki's fingers brush across the columns as casually as a tornado might whip through the American Midwest.

'Nobody knows at this stage how long they're going to be on the trail. They might have a fair idea, but the weather could play up, or you could sprain your ankle. Some people might even move faster than they'd planned,' he says.

'But if something happens . . . they'll know to come and search for us.'

'Think about it. We write down the day we expect to arrive at Melaleuca. Then we don't turn up because the river's burst its banks, leaving us stranded on the other side for a day. Before you know it there'll be rescue helicopters chattering their way out here looking for people that are in no trouble whatsoever.'

'So there actually will be such things, right?'

Jyrki squeezes my shoulder.

'Of course. We'll be crossing rivers and creeks, even a stretch of the sea. There could be strong winds or a freak high tide. You've just got to stay put and stick it out.'

'I meant rescue helicopters.'

Jyrki gives a snort.

We'll be covering our backs, I say.

We'll be smothering our freedom, says Jyrki.

Neither of us says it out loud.

Jyrki leans down towards me; his lips gently touch mine.

'Time to go, babe.'

Babe.

A word that has never once passed his lips before now. Not love, not sweetheart. Nothing.

I look at him and his smile, a smile that exudes a steely inner resolve, a great, burning enthusiasm, penetrating and deliberate.

At some point I started to know that Joseph Conrad book off by heart. It whispers to me.

I wondered whether the stillness on the face of the immensity looking at us two were meant as an appeal or as a menace. What were we who had strayed in here? Could we handle that dumb thing, or would it handle us? I felt how big, how confoundedly big, was that thing that couldn't talk and perhaps was deaf as well. What was in there?

JYRKI

At first the track is the ultimate piece of cake, all duckboards and steps – we'd be lucky to encounter as much as a tree root once every kilometre. I know that the beginning of the trail gives us the wrong impression. The leg from Cockle Creek to the campsite at Lion Rock is clearly cut for people out on a Sunday-afternoon stroll. On the trail we pass plodding retired couples dressed in everyday clothes and shoes and families out on holiday. We even see a couple pushing their kids in a pram, which almost makes me want to cover my head with a paper bag for fear of ending up in a photograph with them.

I take a deep breath. I know this isn't the start of the concert; this isn't even the overture. This is just the murmur of the audience taking their places. That's not the reason we've come all this way. This is just a necessary step we have to take, a stage that has little to do with what's still in store for us. That's when the real show begins.

They were conquerors, and for that you want only brute force — nothing to boast of, when you have it, since your strength is just an accident arising from the weakness of others.

                                            — Joseph Conrad, *Heart of Darkness*

LAPLAND
Levi, the Rabid Reindeer
Saturday, April 2006

HEIDI

The guests were beginning to get pretty wasted. By this point they wanted to see who could drink the others under the table, ordering rounds of vodka shots flavoured with Turkish pepper or Fisherman's Friends and challenging each other to knock them back in one. The atmosphere at the table was loud and raucous. They referred to the alcohol content of their various drinks in 'octane ratings', as though the other customers in the bar hadn't realized from the logos on their college sweaters that the group of revellers worked for an oil company.

The company was the biggest catch our PR firm had reeled in. They had been clients of ours for over two years, and the relationship of trust between us had finally been sealed in a scandal involving the accidental dumping of something unwanted into the Baltic Sea. On an impossibly tight schedule, our team came up with a press release that was such an effective combination of admitting making the mistake in the first place, expressing the necessary level of regret and resolving to improve company procedure – combined with just the right expression of hurt pride ('After all, our company is responsible for alleviating the bulk of the energy burden in Finland's challenging climatic circumstances and, in doing so, plays a vital role in upholding the very infrastructure that supports the wellbeing of our nation . . .') – that what do you know? It's a surprise the company didn't receive a public apology for the damage the scandal had caused them.

As an assistant who had only recently joined the team, I didn't have all that much to do with the success story, but the donation of a substantial sum of money to Greenpeace and the 'accidental' leaking of the story to the press had been my idea. Apparently, the gesture's PR value had played a part in hushing up the fact, much touted by Greenpeace, that the company was buying oil from a supplier drilling in the Yosemite National Park.

According to a recently published study, the image of our oil sheikhs was more glowing than it had been for years – and even a bit greener. Because of our work, every citizen who drives a car or warms their house with an oil burner might feel that their conscience – and perhaps even the environment – was just a little bit cleaner. And it was the triumph of that tiny change in public perception that we had travelled north to celebrate. It was only because this, too, had been my idea (I'd just happened to be bringing coffee into the conference room when the team was talking about it and said something along the lines of 'Hey, never mind a stuffy champers party, we should take them skiing in Lapland for the weekend . . .') that I'd ended up being one of the group of six that was to spend the weekend giving our tanker boys a not-so deserved pat on the back. Because I had the shortest CV, and because I happened to be a woman, I traipsed backwards and forwards to and from the bar as soon as the glasses started to look half empty. Or maybe I'd drawn the short straw because, even though I thought I'd done pretty well in the job so far, everyone seemed a bit too certain that Daddy Dearest had swung me the job in the first place.

Working as a cocktail waitress and trying to stay relatively sober could have mightily pissed me off, but I didn't have a problem with my constant trips to the bar: the bloke behind the counter was a fairly decent specimen. He was almost two metres tall, slim with broad shoulders. His eyes were a light-grey colour, and there was a darker circle around his irises that gave his stare an almost paralysing intensity. No ring on his left hand, but he had a large golden earring dangling at the side of his shiny shaved head. The most impressive thing about him was that he never seemed to make a single unnecessary or unconsidered movement.

I glanced back towards the rabble sitting at our table and tried my best to suppress a shudder. Erkki had given our merry troop very specific instructions to do anything and everything to make sure our guests had a good time. This was one gig that we couldn't afford to screw up, despite the fact that I had noticed Riitta was already displaying obvious signs of tedium.

JYRKI

She was small and nicely proportioned. Black hair flowed evenly down past her shoulders. There was just enough blue in the colour that you could tell some of the tint had come from a bottle. A bit too much sirloin around the rump. A nice pair of apples bobbed on the upper shelf.

Her eyes bore the expression of the most pissed-off person in the world as she appeared at the bar and ordered eight shots of salt-liquorice vodka. She told me they had a tab open. I took the glasses out of the freezer, poured the shots and fished around for the right credit card in a glass on the shelf behind the counter.

I made a joke about how thirsty the young lady must be. She gave an exhausted, crooked smile. By now the racket at the table in the corner had increased as they broke into a round of rowdy drinking songs.

I said I'd bring the shots to the table. I didn't really have the time – the joint was packed, just like every weekend during the skiing-holiday season.

She'd gone back to the table and sat down between two ruddy-faced men. You could tell straight away that they were small-time bosses. Tall good-looking men climb the career ladder at lightning speed. These two, on the other hand, were typical middle-management material, who for years had probably been making up for being vertically challenged with a diet of cutlets, cognac and calling the shots. One of them had put his hand on the back of her chair and sat there panting something in her ear. You could see a mile off that the situation really annoyed her, but there was no way she could reject his advances.

When I put the tray on the table and started handing out the shot glasses, the other red-faced piglet pretended to move out of the way and placed his hand on her thigh. She gave a start, struggling somewhere between politeness and disgust. *Well*, she tapped his hand, *tut tut*, and with that she lifted his paw, in a friendly but firm manner, back on to the table then gave him another companionable tap on the wrist for good measure.

I told them that last orders would be here quicker than they could say Judgement Day and that those who were well prepared would have a far better time than those who hid their talents. This revelation caused a wave of complaints. Not yet, eh? The party's only just getting started. An after party, that's what we need. An after party! The pig-faced bloke put his hand across the backrest of her chair again and started stroking the tips of her dark hair – absentmindedly, apparently. I heard him mutter something about a bottle of cognac that had conveniently found its way up to his hotel room.

She glanced over at me and realized I'd overheard. It may have been only a glance, but I could see a flash of real panic in her eyes.

I remembered something and cleared my throat. I said that the group who had booked the sauna had cancelled at the last minute and that I could make an exception to the rules and give it to them instead. It shouldn't be too hard to get a couple of crates of beer down there, as long as we can come to an agreement about what would be a suitable price. I might even be able to organize some other drinks if the gentlemen fancied having a good long soak. I stressed the word *gentlemen*.

The idea of a sauna gained enthusiastic approval. The hands holding the shot glasses flew up to their mouths like cobras lunging in a chicken hut.

She looked over at me, and I saw I'd made the right move. As the empty shot glasses hit the table in a clacking staccato, she cleared her throat and suggested she could stay here and settle the bill. The older of the two women in the group gave a relieved motherly nod of approval: the idea of the men going to the sauna was wonderful — more than wonderful — the gents would doubtless have plenty of fun on their own, boys will be boys, and they have their manly things to talk about by themselves. She said she would go to the kitchen and ask if they could whip up something savoury to satisfy the masculine appetite — some potato casserole and reindeer sausage maybe.

I saw the look the two women exchanged. They were reading each other's thoughts as though the air were thick with a blizzard of Braille.

Within a few minutes the noise of the plastered posse had disappeared out of the door. After a moment's nodding and dividing up the labour, the older woman finally left the deserted table.

The dark-haired one remained sitting there for a moment amid the chaos of empty shot glasses. She took a breath, stood up and walked straight up to the counter.

Adventure is just a romantic name for trouble.

    – Anonymous philosopher in the registration book at Speargrass Hut

SOUTH COAST TRACK, TASMANIA
Cockle Creek to South Cape Rivulet
Monday, March 2007

HEIDI

It is at Lion Rock that I catch my first glimpse of the southern coastline and get a taste of what it *actually* looks like. After all that park-like landscape, the rugged desolation really takes you aback. New Zealand was one big dramatic postcard, as though a top Italian designer had drawn the landscape on a computer using top-of-the-range software with the aesthetic-maximizer function cranked up. This is different: primitive and rough, so beautiful, in a way I've never seen anywhere else, that at first it's hard to call it beauty at all. The southern coast of Tasmania is beautiful in the same way as the rocky fells of Lapland are beautiful. There's nothing inviting about it, nothing alluring; it's a landscape that is perfectly aware of its own qualities and doesn't feel the need to try to please anyone. It can afford to be aloof. It's like one of those ageing Hollywood stars, Paul Newman, Clint Eastwood, someone whose features have become so layered with the passing of time that no one can really call them handsome any more — let alone beautiful — but whose robust, manly charisma can silence people with its mere presence.

No trees, just ragged undergrowth clinging with teeth-grinding perseverance to the steep, erratically angular cliffs. Further down the ridge, South Cape Bay curves around in a crescent of white sand and black rocks. To the left is the sea; if you were to swim out, your next stop would be in Antarctica.

Although my rucksack is bloody heavy — how can such a small amount of food weigh so much? — at least we've been walking along a fairly level wide path that is clearly well looked after. Just like at Overland, wide duckboards have been built across the damper patches of buttongrass.

I glance at Jyrki. His face is that of a little boy waiting for Father Christmas. Can't you see I'm bursting with the sense of adventure, too, my expression tries to communicate to him.

JYRKI

From Lion Rock onwards the coastal path is treacherous. The strip of shore, cut off on one side by the cliffs, is narrow, rocky and vulnerable to large waves. More than a few ramblers on this leg have been caught off-guard by a freak wave and carried off to sea. Thankfully it's low tide at the moment, and the wind is only moderate. You can just focus on the baking sun, the bracing wind, the billowing sand dunes and the smell of seaweed.

We arrive at South Cape Rivulet well before five o'clock. The campsite is just how I imagined it: right next to the beach on a small strip of land beneath the eucalyptus trees, a number of tent-sized squares have been worn away on the flat areas of terrain and are now covered in several layers of dried leaves.

You could see right off that this was something completely different from Sabine Circuit or Kepler. This was no Overland, let alone Queen Charlotte.

As we trekked along Overland I had heard that slightly off the track there were hidden luxury cabins for organized rambling excursions, complete with indoor toilets, wine cellars and breakfast services.

Overland was a shell, nothing but civilization disguised as wilderness.

Here there are no huts, no cabins, no rangers. There are no foam mattresses, washbasins, water tanks, fireplaces, compost toilets. Soon there probably won't be any mobile-phone signal either. The most luxurious public facility here is the pit toilet, and even they can only be found at designated campsites. The rules concerning rubbish are just as strict, if not even stricter than at Overland. At ecologically sensitive areas you are actually advised to collect your own excrement and take it away with you. At the very least you have to bury it properly. Hiking stores sell special tapered spades for this purpose.

There are already a number of campers here. A group of people rattling their cooking equipment gives us a relaxed wave. More people will doubtless turn up as evening draws in. I examine possible tent sites with a critical eye. I would rather not be shacked up side by side with other people – and preferably not too far from the nearest water source either.

I find a small patch of land next to the beach. A driftwood trunk dragged up on to the shore will make a suitable seat for cooking and eating. There's foliage on three sides to give us some privacy. On the fourth, the sea view opens up before us.

You could almost call it romantic.

I lay my rucksack down against the tree trunk, take an empty water bottle out of the netting on the side and remove the rolled-up Platypus bottle from the upper pocket. Time to go and milk the cows, I tell her.

HEIDI

'That water's really brown.'

Jyrki is already crouching in the brook with the Platypus in his hand. 'It just looks brown; the tea-tree leaves have stained it. In small amounts you don't even notice the difference.'

Jyrki submerges the Platypus and holds its mouth against the current for a moment before pulling it triumphantly into the air as though he had just caught a fish. 'Take a look at that.'

The water in the steamed-up plastic container is still a distinctly yellowy-beige colour. Jyrki looks at it, and the excitement on his face disappears.

'Anyway Tasmania is one of the cleanest places on earth. There's no cattle or farming out here in the middle of Nowheresville – let alone industry or traffic. What could possibly pollute this water? This is perfectly good for drinking. We drank water from the streams at Overland, didn't we?'

He can see my expression and steps out of the brook, water splashing from his hiking boots. 'OK, I admit a kangaroo might have shat in the water. Let's run it through the Katadyn.'

'I believe you,' I say quickly. Jyrki looks at me, nods, lifts the Platypus and drinks, savouring the water in long gulps. I really do believe him; filtering Southern Tasmanian stream water would mean wasting more time and unnecessarily using up the running capacity of an expensive piece of equipment.

Perhaps it would have been easier to accept had the water not come so openly, so brazenly from between Mother Nature's legs.

JYRKI

She's taken off her hiking boots and changed them for her Crocs, and now she says she's hungry.

I take the tent out of its protective bag and unroll it. I hand her a smaller jangling bag and ask her to put the poles together. I explain that we have to put up our house first. This is the first commandment of hiking: the weather can change in an instant, and at times like that having shelter for yourself and your equipment is the first priority.

This is the first time we've put up the tent, although we've been on the road for weeks. Back at Overland Track a tent was part of everyone's required inventory, and so we dutifully lugged it a full sixty-five kilometres without using it once. At Overland the staff restrict the number of hikers to make sure everyone will fit into the huts, although no one can predict how fast individual groups will progress along the route. That's why they insist on a tent, to make sure no one ends up sleeping outdoors, even if the route is furnished with buffed-up huts for lightweights a few hours apart.

Makes you wonder what kind of dopey idiots they've let loose there in the past. Someone must have keeled over with hypothermia after not fitting into a hut and not having the strength to walk a mere two hours; probably took out a threadbare blanket or something and lay down in a snowdrift with predictable results.

She's a fast learner. She manages to work out how the poles fit together and how you slide them into the tunnels without having to be told. I prop up the vestibule and the far end of the outer tent. She fixes the other guy ropes fairly well; I have to adjust only one of the pegs.

She asks whether we can eat now. Again I tell her that first we have to get our home sorted out. After dinner, when we've done all our tasks for the day, at least we'll have something to collapse on. I throw the sleeping-bag, the sleeping-mat and the night bag into the tent and crawl in after them. I ask her at least to zip up the mosquito net if she's going to hang around outside.

She goes to her rucksack to fetch her own things and hurls them through the door. The sleeping-bag hits me; I think that was the point. I manage to catch the sleeping-mat in mid flight, take it out of its bag and open the vents so it can suck in some air. My own mat has already inflated enough to be finished off with a couple of breaths. I place the mat on the left-hand side of the tent and roll out the sleeping-bag on top of it. Then I take the feather travel-pillow out of its compression pack. I neatly lay my thermal underwear and night socks on the pillow. I put the headlamp and the guidebook in the corner pocket at the far end of the tent, along with the map to orientate myself for the next day's leg.

She crawls in beside me and starts clumsily putting her own bed together. We bump into one another again and again. It's only once we start pottering around like this that we realize the tent is pretty small for two people; it's barely wide enough for two to lie down side by side. For one person it has always felt luxuriously spacious.

She says she's ready and asks what we are having for dinner.

I clamber outside and say I'm going to wash myself first. She looks at me for a moment, but we'd already had all these conversations back at Nelson Lakes.

I walk a few metres from the tent to a spot where a thin broken tree trunk rests diagonally against another tree. I hang my civvies and towel over the trunk, take off my clothes and pour water from the Platypus straight over my head. I rub my palms against my cheeks and grunt aloud. I splash my neck, armpits and groin with water. I scrub my hand against my shins, which are now caked in salt and sand dried into the sun-cream and sweat. I can almost see the old dirty, sweaty layers of skin lying wrinkled and pathetic on the bed of eucalyptus leaves beneath my feet.

I pull on my civvies. The air is starting to cool. You only really notice it once you've put on your lounge trousers and a dry long-sleeved shirt. She comes out of the tent carrying her own stuff, tight-lipped. From the cargo pocket on her shorts she takes out a small bottle with water she's carried all the way from Cockle Creek.

The bottle originally came from the aeroplane. It was lying on its side on the Qantas dinner tray. The bottle is round and angular, like a small, chubby whisky flask. She decided to call it the wombat bottle the first time she saw some swollen cubes of wombat shit on the duckboards at Overland. As the wombat's shit so uncannily resembles the shape of the animal that made it, she decided the design aesthetics of this bottle clearly must have had something to do with wombats, too.

My first thought is, Jesus Christ, she won't even wash herself with the brown stream water; that's why she's taken out the bottle. Then I get it. The sun and her thigh have been warming that water all day. The wombat bottle holds about a quarter of a litre of water – a generous amount for washing yourself at the camp. By now it's probably warm to the touch.

Damn, she's not giving up. It almost makes me smile.

She crouches down to wash herself but doesn't wet her head. She might as well: her half-centimetre crop, which sometimes makes her look like a little Latino boy, would dry in no time. She pours water over her neck and back, letting it run into her armpits. She keeps her Crocs on her feet, just like I did: wet feet will only gather up more crap. With water in the palm of her hand, she splashes her groin, then stands up and dries herself on a sarong.

She pulls on her civvies and hangs up her hiking socks, shorts and T-shirt to dry. The sarong is left flapping on the fallen tree. I've already taken out the camp kettle.

'How about some super-delicious chicken noodles?' I ask.

Heidi

This is the first time I've slept in a sleeping-bag in years. I'd forgotten how claustrophobic it can be. I'd forgotten what it feels like not being able to poke your toes out of the end of the duvet, not being able to move your legs properly from side to side and how difficult it is trying to turn on to your side or stomach.

As I lie awake and listen to the sea, I realize that I'd also forgotten just how thin a piece of fabric it is that separates me from the night outside.

And in the hush that had fallen suddenly upon the whole sorrowful land, the immense wilderness, the colossal body of the fecund and mysterious life seemed to look at her, pensive, as though it had been looking at the image of its own tenebrous and passionate soul.

— Joseph Conrad, *Heart of Darkness*

LAPLAND
Levi, the Rabid Reindeer
Sunday, April 2006

HEIDI

It was a bizarre-looking concoction to say the least, with layers of clear and red liquid.

I wanted to ask what the hell was in the glass but decided instead just to knock it back in one.

Wow.

At first my taste buds didn't know quite how to react, then a split second later my mouth was filled with a most extraordinary sensation and my arms were covered in goosebumps.

'What the . . . ?'

'Sambuca and tomato juice.'

Well, I suppose I had asked him to come up with something to help alleviate my acute symptoms of fatigue, irritation and of being far too sober.

I reached into my handbag and dug out my wallet. 'Let's not put this on the company card. Our accountant's really anal about this kind of stuff. A bloke in our office once ordered a packet of peanuts in a club, and the accountant made him list exactly which clients had eaten them – all that for some point-less expenses clause.'

He put his finger on my wallet and pushed it back towards me. 'On the house.'

'Can you do that?'

'That's what the write-off book is for.'

I started to laugh. It felt as though the weird and wonderful drink had taken the lift from my palate right up to my brain, where it had come to rest and was now giving off a soothing, numbing glow.

'Thanks . . .' I paused, meaningfully.

'Jyrki.'

'Thanks, Jyrki.' I reached my hand across the counter and watched and above all *felt* the way his enormous fist swallowed it up. 'Heidi.'

'And is Heidi having another one?'

'She certainly is.'

JYRKI

It's normally fun closing up the bar. You can play God for a moment and flick the lights for last orders. Then you turn from Jekyll into Hyde: just a minute ago I was smiling, joking, genially pouring fresh drinks, then in a flash I transform into a humourless, monosyllabic tightarse. In seconds the generous provider, everyone's best friend, the life and soul of the party, is transformed into a cold-hearted thrower-outer.

Still, the last-orders bell doesn't mean your shift's over. There are still glasses, drinks measures and beer trays to rinse out. You have to make an inventory of the day's takings, reset the credit-card machine, then clear up all the shards of broken glass and pieces of lemon rind on the floor behind the counter.

But on that one occasion I allowed the bar to remain open a little longer. The shift manager had told me to use my common sense when it came to closing time, so long as we stayed within the letter of the law. I made a judgement call: I was only too happy to carry on looking at that black fountain of hair and the glinting expression behind that thick even fringe – a look that was a mixture of exhaustion and mischief, caution and seduction, sweet and savoury. It wasn't for nothing I'd given her that sambuca-and-tomato-juice shot: it was barman's instinct.

I poured her another one every time she emptied her glass.

HEIDI

The coffee filter was rinsed out, the bottles counted, and the whirring cash register was busy churning out an endless stream of receipts. Jyrki's movements seemed minimal, but everything happened as if by magic. Every now and then he would stop to exchange a few words and didn't seem to want to encourage me to drink up the last in a seemingly continuous line of shots that had appeared in front of me – although many of the other customers nodding off in their chairs were told politely but firmly that perhaps it was time to hit the hay.

Jyrki was quite a catch, I thought as my brain turned gradually softer and softer.

I learnt that he was originally from Ostrobothnia and now lived in Tampere

– or at least that was where his official address was – but that his flat was a small, cheap rented bedsit which he only really used to store his stuff.

Jyrki was on the books of some staffing agency that hired him out and sent him off all over Finland. There was always a need for experienced bar staff: holiday cover, summer festivals, city festivals, rock festivals, new bars opening up that wanted to get things off the ground with staff that knew what they were doing. There was plenty of work, and he was often able to pick and choose between offers. The local employer generally sorted him out with accommodation, usually a shared flat or some other modest place suitable for a free spirit with no wife or kids.

'The winter season is the best round here. The summer's grim. You should see those slopes when there's no snow.'

I'd never thought of that.

'So you've been here in the summer, too?'

'In the autumn. Been hiking a bit out in the fells.'

A barman with a rucksack? Wow.

'We're like modern-day lumberjacks. We'll go wherever there's work. Winter in Lapland, summer at the Seinäjoki Tango Festival, the Hanko Regatta, Kaustinen or wherever . . . And, besides, during the summer you always need staff to serve in all the beer gardens.'

'*I'm a lumberjack, and I'm OK . . .*' I burst into song.

Jyrki gave a laugh.

'I had a different song in mind.' Then, in a voice – a grave, profound, vibrating voice: '*Gladly we rushed there, where the common calling rang . . .*'

I was in raptures.

'*Our steps have the same echo!*'

'*All the way from Hanko to Petsamo!*'

Our old Second World War march was brusquely interrupted by someone who was apparently Jyrki's boss. He scowled at us, said something tight-lipped about closing up the bar and washing out some blender or other. Jyrki smiled at me and shrugged his shoulders as if to say, What can I do? From the other end of the counter, his dexterous hands taking some machine apart, he turned to me and raised his eyebrows in a look that really got my juices flowing.

I downed the last drops of tomato and aniseed.

Shit.

'And a very good night to you, too,' the puffed-up boss said from behind the bar, looking meaningfully right at me.

I slammed the glass on the counter and walked towards the door, doubtless staggering more than a bit. The sub-zero air outside was bracing and fresh, and the blue-black sky seemed oppressively beautiful.

Someone was standing by the stairwell having a cigarette – a member of staff at the Rabid Reindeer, to judge by the shirt.

'Sorry, do you know a barman called Jyrki?' I asked in passing.

The man looked at me suspiciously.

All of its own accord, the story started bubbling convincingly from my mouth. Such excellent service, blah blah blah, then before we knew it the bar had closed, Jyrki had disappeared, and my boss Riitta had wanted to give him a special tip, a personal one, a big one. She'd told me to give it to him. In person.

JYRKI

It was half past four in the morning. I'd just got back to my room when someone started hammering on the door.

I furrowed my brow in confusion but went to open it.

It was the girl from the bar. Her dark hair was a bit tousled. You could tell from her eyes that all those sambuca shots had finally hit her bloodstream.

She wanted to talk. Because we'd only just got started.

I asked her how she knew where I lived.

She said she'd worked it out.

I told her I was about to go to bed.

She said she'd be more than happy to come to bed, too, and ducked under my arm and into the room. She sat down on the edge of the bed and started unbuttoning her blouse, although she still had her shoes on.

She was endearingly tipsy.

I let her undress to see just how serious she was.

She was deadly serious.

Without her clothes on, her body was worthy of more serious attention.

I folded her clothes and laid them on a chair. I sat next to her on the bed and tried to focus on her hopeful, slightly blurry eyes, although my own kept scanning downwards almost by force. I gently pushed her shoulders and lowered her on to her back. Her lips were set in a pout, waiting expectantly to be kissed.

I took the bedspread and pulled it over her.

I told her it wasn't really my style to screw anyone who wasn't a hundred per cent sure what they were doing, but that if she felt the same way in the morning we could renegotiate.

The next morning she felt exactly the same way. Still.

HEIDI

I left Jyrki's room with only a few minutes to spare before our brunch appointment with the clients.

Jyrki had told me he had the day off.

At brunch I was bubbly and euphoric, and although I'd had a shower – my hair was still damp, a detail Riitta surely didn't fail to pick up on – I was certain that I must have given off the pungent scent of multiple satiation.

Erkki twice pointed out that a client was speaking to me. I giggled, flicked my hair, pouted and laughed it off.

But beneath the surface I was seething. Christ alive. I'd wanted a one-night stand. I'd had a one-night stand.

I'd had an *exceptionally high-quality* one-night stand.

And not only that: I'd met a man with principles.

What's more, on the way I'd succeeded in painting myself into a corner.

The rules of interaction between man and woman, between hunter and prey, are eternal. If the hunter is interested, the prey calls the shots.

When I decided to turn from prey into hunter, I turned control of the situation over to Jyrki.

I craved for a resumption of our little fling so much that my heart ached, and my body seemed to be splitting itself into two climatic regions, one of which was rather tropical. But what sort of woman goes and throws herself at the same guy twice? Say no more . . .

What if I just swallowed my pride and risked rejection?

This was such a painful possibility that I didn't even want to entertain the idea – a matter that wasn't remotely entertaining. The choice would be his. That's the way it is.

As I sat in the women's loo during our brunch, which had extended well into the afternoon, I had to dig into my handbag, take out my wallet and stuff it between my teeth to make sure my miserable, frustrated whimpering couldn't be heard in the adjacent cubicle, leaving a series of deep crescents impressed into the brown nappa leather.

At dinner later that evening, it was barely ten o'clock when I complained of a headache, made my apologies and left the table, my glass of cognac untouched.

I went back to my room and switched on the television.

I had to keep my resolve.

Still, I wasn't entirely surprised when, half an hour later, there came a knock at the door.

And no, it wasn't Riitta bringing me a Nurofen.

The doorbell rang. Might have been Tuesday.

Didn't answer. Probably the Jehovahs or something. If somebody wants me they can call, and if someone calls it's up to me whether I answer.

It doesn't matter what time you open your eyes. The air's the same: grey and grainy. From the light you can tell day from night. If you want to.

It's night when the streetlamps shine a stain on the floor.

It's day when the stain isn't there.

It's summer when there's a stain there all the time.

The quilt's sticky and too hot. If I throw it off, soon I'm too cold as the sweat chills against my skin. Crappy quilt, too thick. Could sleep with just a sheet if I had one. I think there's one in the bathroom, in a heap in a corner. So many stains on it that it's stiff in places. Blood and cum; some mine, some other people's. Or maybe the blood's not mine. Or maybe it is. I get nosebleeds.

The grainy air is fizzing in front of my eyes. It could be any time of day.

The good thing about winter is you can sleep whenever you like for as long as you like.

SOUTH COAST TRACK, TASMANIA
South Cape Rivulet to Surprise Bay
Tuesday, March 2007

HEIDI

It might be too late by the time we leave South Cape Bay, or so I've already heard Jyrki mention several times as he glances at his chunky multifunction watch. Clearing out the camp took much longer than setting it up, and the moment we step out of the camp and on to the sands along the beach I realize that we're late. Crucially late.

South Cape Rivulet is shallow, sometimes nothing more than a creek. It was from the side next to the beach, flowing out from the depths of the impenetrable thicket, that we had collected our drinking water the previous evening. As it flows towards the sea the current cuts across the sands at the bottom of the bay, forming a channel a couple of metres wide. Hikers normally just wade right through it, no problem, to reach the other side where South Coast Track – or Southy, as Jyrki has already started to call it affectionately – continues on its way towards Granite Beach. The water reaches up to your knees.

At low tide.

By now the rivulet is wide and deep, although through the brown water you can't see quite how deep. To me it almost seems like the work of some malevolent magic. I can understand how the rivers flood in Ostrobothnia when the snow melts in the spring or during the monsoon season in tropical regions, but how a river can widen and deepen so dramatically twice a day is beyond my comprehension. It's almost as though it's breathing in horrifically slow motion.

Jyrki looks out at the strengthening current and sighs.

'We'll never get across,' I hear myself say, my voice shaking, perhaps even with something approaching relief.

Jyrki puts his rucksack down on the sands, secures his hiking poles beneath the side straps, and in a single uninterrupted motion proceeds to untie the laces of his hiking boots, take off his socks, stuff them inside the boots and tie the laces together in an overband knot. Then he strips off his shorts, his T-shirt and even his underwear without batting an eyelid.

I can't help but look back towards the edge of the camp, but the border of eucalyptus trees is like a green botanic wall.

A similar wall faces us on the other side of the rivulet. No, that one's far darker and thicker, rising up along the high green rocky embankment.

The woods were unmoved, like a mask — heavy, like the closed door of a prison — they looked with their air of hidden knowledge, of patient expectation, of unapproachable silence.

Oh, Joseph, Joseph.

'They've seen naked men before, and if they haven't it's about time they did,' Jyrki says. He stuffs his clothes beneath the strap of his rucksack and tightens the buckle to form a secure bundle. He hangs his boots around his neck so that they are dangling across his chest, one on each side, picks his rucksack up from the sand and places it on his head. The naked man then steps into the current.

The channel deepens so suddenly that after only two steps Jyrki is up to his waist in water. Another step and the water almost reaches up to his chest; the soles of the boots dangling around his neck skim the surface of the rivulet. A step further and the water is once again at his waist, then his thighs, his shins. Jyrki throws his rucksack and boots on to the sand on the opposite shore and without a moment's hesitation gets back into the water.

'Strip off if you don't want to trudge around in wet clothes for the rest of the day.'

'The water'll be up to my neck.'

'Swim. Head diagonally into the current. It's pretty strong; you can feel it in your legs.'

'How strong?'

My clothes fall on to the sand; my hands are trembling. Jyrki crosses the rivulet in an instant and stands there naked in front of me, water dripping on to the ground. He takes my boots, which I haven't had time to tie together, and throws them one at a time across the water. I hear a dull thud as they hit the sand. Jyrki snatches up my clothes and hiking poles, stuffs them under the straps around my rucksack, and with a single graceful pull he has the whole heavy load perfectly balanced on his head as though he were a robust native woman of some exotic country. He wades out into the brown water, reaches the opposite shore before I can take more than a few tentative steps and throws my rucksack on to the sand. Then he turns around and holds out his hand, a living bridge, and I don't even need to see whether my feet can touch the bottom as he's already pulling me towards the other side, steering me along the surface like a child.

*

Tasmania shows us its true colours the minute we cross the rivulet, as if it knew that after all that dressing and undressing and wallowing around in the potentially life-threatening current we wouldn't be turning back any time soon.

This is the point of no return, it seems to be telling us.

Just climbing up the muddy, stony embankment from South Cape Bay is worse than anything we've seen in Tasmania so far. After that we head straight into a thick, damp forest, every now and then reaching clearings dotted with clumps of buttongrass that we have to negotiate. From there we descend creeks fed by networks of brown streams into the tangle of shadowy copses, then up again, this time to a series of rocky ridges. After that we are engulfed by steep stony inclines, the thicket and the darkness of the rainforest.

The path is nothing but a zigzagging trail of sloppy, shitty sludge. Up and down, then down and up we go — mostly up, of course, clambering up infuriatingly steep slippery banks. For a bit of variety sometimes we have to slide down the hillside or some tree roots on our arses, simply because our legs aren't long enough or the path has no steps, all the while wrenching our rucksacks free of the bush and scrub, hauling our boots out of the smacking mud and prying our hiking poles from between the rocks with all our strength. Endlessly.

If Australia is mostly bone dry, this part of Tasmania seems to be nothing but a thin layer of land above a deep heaving quagmire. The crème brûlée of terrains, I'll bloody tell you. And over the years hundreds of hiking boots have cracked the surface, opening up fissures like black greedy mouths for kilometres ahead.

At the highest point of South Cape Range, about 450 metres up — Jyrki makes a point of mentioning the specific height, as though it were of some special significance — we start our descent towards Granite Beach. Despite the effort, it's impossible not to notice the sheer grandeur of the landscape spreading out before us. Some way off, far down the hillside, I can see an overgrown peninsula that we still have to cross, and the sandy, rocky coves extending in an endless series of crescents into the distance. Prion Beach, the place Jyrki keeps mentioning, can apparently just be made out — maybe it's that dull-golden cuticle-shaped strip on the horizon. I can see the lines of foaming waves hitting the beach, the turquoise water, and I'd like to think how beautiful it is.

You can't argue with that.

Even though every part of my body is aching, I have to admit that Tasmania is in some unfathomable way both age-old and fresh as the day it was born. Old and experienced enough that it knows how to touche a nerve but at the same time so young that it almost feels as though we are depriving a newborn creature of the peace is has just discovered and needs.

The bushes rustle and crackle – always to the left, always behind us, incessantly – as though Tasmania itself were following us, invisible, smart enough constantly to devise little pranks and childish enough to carry them out.

JYRKI

The three guys that left Cockle Creek at the same time as us have decided to spend the night at Granite Beach. They've already put their tents up. Their sweaty T-shirts are flapping in the trees. I look at my watch.

She's about to take her rucksack off when I show her the map. It's less than two hours to Surprise Bay. Half of the journey is along Granite Beach. I mean, a *beach*, for God's sake – what could be nicer than that? Then all we have to do is cross that peninsula and we'll be there – Surprise, Surprise – just in time for dinner.

She asks what's wrong with this place.

There's nothing wrong with it, I say, but we'd have to make up the ground tomorrow. It's only another four or five kilometres. We've got ten behind us, so that will make fifteen for the day. If we stay here it'll be another twenty-one kilometres to Deadman's Bay. And we have to factor in crossing the river. This'll even out our daily stretches.

I don't tell her that according to the guidebook it should be a twenty-one-kilometre leg split in two with an overnight stay at Osmidirium Beach. But that would mean one of the legs would be only three or four hours long. A complete waste of a day, in other words.

Another group of travel writers that hasn't bothered thinking things through properly.

HEIDI

Ten kilometres?

Ten kilometres behind us?

You're having a laugh. Ten kilometres in *seven hours*. Seven hours of unrelenting hellish, desperate trudging and scrambling, and it's got us only *ten kilometres?* In New Zealand we were doing almost thirty kilometres in the same time.

Oh, *only* another four or five kilometres?

When we reach the place where we're supposed to descend towards the beach I find it hard to contain my desire to scream.

Beneath us is an almost sheer drop, ten metres high. Attached to a gnarled tree and the rocks is a frayed-looking blue-and-green nylon rope dangling down the jagged cliff face.

'No.' I hear my hollow voice rising from the bottom of my lungs.

Jyrki either doesn't hear me or pretends not to hear me.

'Are you going first or shall I?' he asks.

It's a rhetorical question; he's already let go of his hiking poles, which are now dangling on the end of his arms by their wrist straps, and tugs at the rope to check that it'll hold.

'It'll be easier for you to come down when I'm there to help you.'

Jyrki takes hold of the rope, wraps it around his right arm for added support, then starts lowering himself backwards down the slope. OK, it's not exactly a sheer drop – now that he's started moving downwards you can see it slopes a bit – but it's still bloody steep.

Jyrki only occasionally looks down at his feet – choosing instead to rely more on the rope itself and wedge the points of his boots into the small fissures in the rock – and descends the slope as nimbly as a monkey, jumping the last couple of feet to the ground. His rucksack yanks him backwards, forcing him to take a few steps to steady his balance.

'Right then.'

I take two deep breaths and pick up the rope as gingerly as if it were a venomous snake. I decide to copy Jyrki and wrap it around my arm for extra security and grip the nylon rope so tightly that I can feel it digging into my fingers. I back up towards the edge of the cliff and, with my right leg fumbling around, start to make my descent.

'Over there, there. One centimetre to your left.' I can hear Jyrki's voice from below. I move my foot slightly to the left and find that there is, after all, a small tongue of rock beneath my foot to take my weight. 'Right, and another, straight down, a bit more. There you go.' And with that the grooves on the bottom of my left boot find something to latch on to. 'Then the next one, a bit further to the right, good. Now move your hands down the rope. You're doing fine.'

I'm soaked with sweat by the time I feel someone taking hold of my hips – those strong arms, their firm grip on both sides of my hipbone.

'Jump.'

I release the rope and land on Granite Beach. It's almost as if I'd arrived on the surface of the moon, Jyrki's hands helping me to defy gravity for a brief moment. I look up, and the slope I have just come down seems to rise halfway up into the sky.

Granite Beach. A beach, for God's sake. What could be nicer than that? Yeah, right.

This 'beach' consists of boulders, eroded by the sea into more or less spherical blocks varying from the size of a child's head to that of a widescreen television.

The path forces you to balance on and between the rocks because there is simply no alternative: on one side there is the ocean; on the other the steep cliff face. And because the tide flushes and moves these boulders on a daily basis they're not firmly fixed in one place, so they constantly wobble, rolling and clunking beneath your boots. The tide is coming in now, too, the waves washing against the shore, slamming the rocks against one another only a few metres away from us. Our poles are no use either, as they just skim across the curved surfaces of the boulders with a grating screech and end up stuck in between them. It would be suicide to rely on your poles here; at best they are only a half-decent indicator of how wobbly the next stone is.

The rucksack's centre of balance somehow always feels wrong; the stone that looks stable wavers the most. I look between the boulders and think of them as giant meat mincers. That's what they are: if your leg slips down there and your own weight comes crashing down on to the rock, your shin and thigh bones would be smashed with a convincing crunch.

If your leg gets stuck down there, the next thing to contend with would be the tide.

Every muscle in your body has to be alert. Every fraction of every second you have to be aware of all the possible vectors and trajectories that the fine balance between your rucksack and your leg, the stone and your weight, might draw through the air, as you balance there between your body and the surface of the rock.

Hop! Jump over! Don't fall! Leap as soon as you feel yourself stumbling!

Anticipate that feeling of 'Oh my God, I'm going to lose my balance' . . . Then hop again!

When a more level stretch of sand comes into view and every muscle is reeling from the constant exertion, there comes an almost religious sense of relief upon finding a real, glorious pathway. And it's only once that path is finally underfoot that the knowledge that this means well over two hours of trudging through the undulating valley-hill-creek-lowland terrain slowly begins to seep up to your brain. That and the fact that the setting sun will be relentlessly and malevolently beating down on you every step of the way.

Dripping with sweat, I crouch down in one of the relatively few brooks here that are shaded by the overhanging bushes; I'm beyond caring about getting my arse wet – so long as there's shade and water. Water. I scoop it right into my mouth without giving a flying fuck about its colour.

The air is buzzing with enormous flies, so large and fleshy that you wouldn't want to swat them: you can just imagine their insides oozing something nameless and disgusting.

Thankfully our final uphill stretch before arriving at Surprise Beach is almost shady, and the sun is already so low in the sky that it doesn't burn directly down upon us.

Once the tent's been put up, the beds laid out and we've had a wash, it's already dusk, and I want nothing more than to consume something and to collapse.

He desired to have kings meet him at railway-stations on his return from some ghastly Nowhere, where he intended to accomplish great things.

— Joseph Conrad, *Heart of Darkness*

HELSINKI
September 2006

HEIDI

Jyrki had taken a temporary job helping to set up a trendy new nightclub for the rich and famous in Helsinki. He had the day off, and we were sitting in the Bruuveri Bar sipping local microbrewery ale when he dropped his bombshell.

'Six months, give or take. Departure around Christmas time when it's the height of summer down under, then back here before the beer gardens open for the season. January in New Zealand, then on to the hiking routes along the Australian coast and maybe even Tasmania; then in March, when it starts getting cooler, back to mainland Australia for some bushwalking in the outback. Then in April maybe fly to the States, go to the Appalachians and trek until the summer. You'll only need a tourist visa for the couple of months there.'

'Six months?'

'When you travel that far, you might as well go round the world. For some fucked-up reason it works out cheaper that way.'

Bloody hell, the man was deadly serious.

'And spend the whole time in the bush?'

Jyrki nodded. 'Of course, you have to move from one place to the next and work out public-transport connections to the different tracks and all the rest of it, so spending the odd day in town is unavoidable. But there are plenty of backpackers in New Zealand and Australia; cheap accommodation is an industry all of its own. You can get a berth in a hostel for twenty bucks or so.'

He described the typical backpackers' hostel: dormitories with shared kitchen and facilities. If you wanted to throw some money around you could book into a private double room, and for real luxury some places even had en-suite rooms, but they cost almost as much as a cheap hotel. Jyrki would be happy with the dormitory.

He had been saving up for two years. Even with the skiing season in Lapland there was always less work during the winter. If he wanted to take a long holiday, it made perfect sense to do it over the winter months.

The solution to the winter-hiking dilemma was simple: although the thought of the carbon emissions from a flight to the other side of the world was cause for serious concern, he had always wanted to visit the Antipodes. He had asked his staffing agency some cautious questions to test the water and to determine whether his taking for six months off would cause them a headache of astronomical proportions, but apparently he would always be welcome back on their list.

Operation Down Under, he'd started to call it.

There was something about his distinctly uncharacteristic display of garrulousness that gave me the feeling something unpleasant was just around the corner. And, believe me, it was.

He offered to give me back my freedom.

It sounded like a line from a Victorian novel. A man and a woman have entered into a hasty engagement, it will be years before they can get married – not before the groom has been ordained or the bride received her family inheritance. More to the point, one or both of them realizes that they have made a terrible mistake, and, even though it would be rather scandalous in the eyes of society at large, the only way to avoid the marriage would be to offer to give the bride back her 'freedom'.

Didn't he want to keep me waiting for six months?

Either this was a way of showing you really cared about someone, or it was the complete opposite.

Paranoia set in straight away: could someone really come up with such a far-fetched scheme as nothing but a smokescreen, a seemingly honourable way out of a relationship that had started to bore him?

Jyrki had said he enjoyed being with me specifically because I hadn't tried to tie him down or restrict him too much. I hadn't insisted on him settling down, let alone suggested moving in together.

On my part it hadn't even been a tactical move. It suited me just fine that we saw each other when we could and when we felt like it. Or so I'd thought.

In any case, clinging on to someone out of a sense of duty was never my idea of a functional relationship; I'd seen enough of that at home before my mother finally upped and left.

There couldn't be someone else, could there? Bloody hell.

It wouldn't have surprised me. Jyrki met legions of women every day, most of them dressed up to the nines, out looking for company – and drunk. He had told me he never took advantage of that particular perk of the job and that I'd been the exception that proved the rule. Of course, he could just have been spinning me a line.

I had to know, and there was only one way to find out.

I looked at him coyly from behind my eyelashes.

'You haven't even asked if I want go with you,' I heard myself saying.

JYRKI

I had to laugh. It wasn't exactly polite of me.

Her lower eyelids rose up across her eyes, the lashes almost catching on one another. I remembered some of the stories she had told me, how she'd had to fight at work not to be seen as the girl who makes the coffee or the girl who does the photocopying just because she was the young and pretty new recruit; how she had to prove that she had brains, too.

Brains, yes — but guts and stamina? The idea of her coming along hadn't even crossed my mind. But when I gave it a moment's consideration, it didn't seem all that crazy after all.

Travelling the world in pairs has its advantages. You don't have to carry all your stuff with you every time you go anywhere; the other one can stay behind and keep an eye on things. Dividing the load means having to carrying much less: we would sleep in the same tent, share the same cooking equipment, the same toiletries and first-aid kit and the hefty guidebooks and maps.

We'd known each other for a couple of months. We hadn't exactly practised living together, if you don't count spending the odd night at one another's flat. Because I didn't know where I'd be working from one day to the next, the idea of settling into a traditional relationship took some getting used to. Perhaps I was more a 'girl in every port' kind of guy.

But as I started getting more and more work in the capital and around southern Finland, before we knew it we'd started acting like a couple. A few times I'd even deliberately chosen a gig down this way instead of somewhere in Mikkeli or Joensuu. After all, why not? On the face of it she had all the right credentials: she was smart enough and quite a tiger between the sheets. But how would we get along shoulder to shoulder, quite literally, twenty-four-seven?

She flicked her thick dark hair, and I tried to imagine her ponytail stuffed beneath a baseball cap. I wasn't convinced she knew quite what she was getting herself into. Women normally have a fit at the idea of not having an opportunity to wash their hair for a week.

HEIDI

I had learnt long ago that there was more to Jyrki than met the eye – an ever-so slightly arrogant, exceptionally good-looking cocktail waiter. He had spent several years studying art and media in Tampere. He'd taken a summer job at a pub owned by a friend of a friend and decided that he liked being face to face with a random flow of people. When the friend's pub closed down he had registered with a staffing agency and started working across the country. It was then that he discovered his inner nomad, as he put it, and realized that working as a barman was the perfect way to combine a life on the move with practical social psychology – his words, not mine.

Jyrki's days as a student had given him a very wide general knowledge, and he was frighteningly well read.

I waited, my pulse on overdrive, my hands cold.

Hands. Jyrki's enormous, warm hands that with such magical dexterity and intoxicating assurance knew just how to touch every part of me. Soon those hands would be on the other side of the globe.

So would that shaven head, that forehead behind which there lurked a momentary understanding of me; that and his astonishing ability to read people, something that caught me off-guard time after time.

Suddenly a chunk of my life would be left completely empty. A gap that I thought I'd already filled.

The thought of that loss gnawed at me, pained me; I knew that beneath Jyrki's cool, statuesque exterior there was a fire burning that could rival Yellow-stone. It was Jyrki who had first told me about it, the supervolcano beneath Yellowstone, which sooner or later would destroy the planet, smothering it in fire and ash – if we humans hadn't managed to do it first, that is.

And as I sat there, my hands trembling, pretending to blow the froth on my microbrewery pint, I wondered what the hell I'd do if he said yes.

I'd already talked to Erkki and Riitta about my input at the PR company, and they'd both said that I'd done really well and that if I did another few supplementary courses at the marketing institute I could start taking on clients of my own. There was no question that I'd be able to continue working for the oil-company team. 'We've had some very good feedback about you,' Erkki had said in passing, and I couldn't help but wince when I thought of who had given him that feedback: the brand manager Antti-Pekka; it must have been him, the one with a face as round as the full moon and a pair of paws that he found very hard to keep to himself.

I could forget all about this if I told them I'd be disappearing for six months. I could probably forget about my job, too. I'd done really well, but I still had a long way to go before I would be considered indispensible.

Then an icy avalanche flowed into my stomach.

Dad.

I tried to imagine his voice roaring like a lion down the telephone when he heard. And he would hear about it straight away. Dad was a friend of one of our bosses from the Lions Club, the same boss he'd done his best to sweeten up before I was offered an internship.

He'd kill me. I mean, really kill me.

And the flat. There was no way I'd have enough money to keep it empty. And, besides, for a trip like that you need money, shit loads of money. The last time I'd borrowed money from Daddy Dearest was for the deposit on the flat, and it had been so humiliating that I'd sworn it would be the last time. The moment he heard about me leaving my job the family coffers would be locked shut for ever.

A banker's draft? A loan? And who would guarantee it?

I understood immediately that there was no point mentioning any of these problems to Jyrki. Discussion of the matter would be shut down straight away.

But I really wanted to see this through. This was a chance to do something for once. By myself. For myself. Well, almost by myself but without Dad's helping hand in my face everywhere I went – in more ways than one.

When Mum left and we stayed with Dad, the words I heard most frequently from his mouth went something along the lines of 'A spoilt little brat like you will never make anything of yourself in the world.'

Makes you wonder who did the spoiling.

If I did this, nobody would be able to order me around or tell me what to do ever again.

And just then, with the inevitable logic of a dream, part of everything that I wanted to put behind me materialized right before my eyes.

JYRKI

A guy in his early twenties approached our table. Not washing his hair for a week was clearly not a problem for him. He was dressed in provocative baggy trousers, and the smile on his face was probably supposed to be one of friendly condescension but succeeded in looking as grim as a framed rictus of agony.

She noticed the approaching kid straight away and tried to avoid contact by pretending to look around but soon realized that he was walking towards us with all the determination and tact of an oncoming tram.

He parked himself by our table, leaning backwards with mock self-assurance, and said something that was a mixture of familiarity and disdain. She stared at the table and grunted almost inaudibly. Everything about the kid's body language said he was doing this just to torment her; the lack of any genuine desire to talk to one another was painfully obvious.

The punk's eyes lit up like traffic lights: first came the rejection, then the need for revenge and finally the spark of glee that might result from his upcoming counterattack. A hand appeared out of his pocket, and he thrust it towards me. I heard something along the lines of 'I don't think we've met. Hi, I'm Heidi's brother Jesse.'

I had to take hold of the paw and say my name, although the kid had made it clear the formality was just another way of taking the piss. I made our brief handshake firm enough that he should have spent the next minute or so blowing on his knuckles. After composing himself for a second, the conversation continued with a comment sucked through clenched teeth:

'Jyrki, mate, I thought you'd have higher standards in the girlfriend department.'

I looked at her. Her head was drooping, her black hair hiding her eyes at the sides.

I looked at the little twat, smiling as broadly as I could muster.

'Funny you should say that,' I said. 'We've just decided to go off to New Zealand and Australia together. For months. Far away from this sleety shithole of a country.'

The kid's eyes betrayed a look that told me the revelation had really hit the spot. No real answer came out of his throat. Stammering a pathetic 'Good luck, mate', the wannabe macho man left the table, walking in an absurdly laboured wide gait, presumably in an attempt to look cool.

She raised her eyes from the tabletop and noticed that he'd gone.

'So that's your little bro,' I said.

She nodded.

'Not exactly on the best of terms,' I said.

She shook her head.

'So what does our young Jesse do then?' I asked.

'Nothing.'

Can't be arsed to get up, but find just enough energy to throw back the quilt and have a slash in the bog.

Sometimes you just can't see the point and let it out in the bed, then crawl away from the wet patch. It was only an old rubber-foam mattress. It didn't matter. I chucked it out when it started to stink too much. The old man gave me money for a new one when I told him a mate had burnt holes in it with a smoke.

The old man muttered something about what sort of mates go around trashing other people's stuff, and I said he's a bit sick in the head. He fell for it, just like he'd done that time we'd put all that grit along the skiing tracks. People coming down at full tilt, then they struck that grit and then they were really in the shit. You should've fucking seen 'em fly. Somebody seen us, but he couldn't pin it on us. I said it was Ante. Ante said it was Kenu. Kenu said it was me, and we stuck to our story and didn't change it, and all of a sudden they couldn't pin it on us.

We'd thought about tying a fishing line across the slope. But 'cos of the height of people's necks and the position they're in and all that, the line would just hit them on the forehead or the chest. We'd talked about one of the roads that were popular with the moped boys. They're going along at a nice speed, their height's always about the same and they'll never see that fishing line coming.

There's stuff in the fridge, but nothing takes my fancy. The old man pays my shopping bills. The cashier's got instructions not to sell me beer or smokes on credit. Sometimes I buy loads of packets of coffee. You can make a bit of easy money off them. But pushing coffee is just a pastime, and it's not like I need the money. I don't understand money. You need shit loads of it to make any real difference to your life. No matter how much you work, you're still never going to have your own private jet.

I don't care whether my flat has one room or two, so long as it don't leak inside. Too much space just causes you extra hassle. I'm fine in the spring when the sun stain arrives. I gather up all the empty burger cartons and pizza boxes and take 'em out to the bin. Things living in 'em.

It's a while yet till the sun stain comes, and it makes me think of those two twats traipsing about in the back of fucking beyond in some fucking part of Aus-fucking-tralia. That's where the sun is now, shining down on 'em, koalas and kangaroos all around. That's where they'll be, frazzling their skin. The Princess and the fucking Peahead.

What the hell are they trying to prove?

SOUTH COAST TRACK, TASMANIA
Surprise Bay
Tuesday, March 2007

JYRKI

We've got the luxury of being here by ourselves. For the first night in my life, for kilometre after kilometre, there isn't a single homo sapiens around that I haven't chosen to be with.

Because of our extra stretch we're almost a whole day ahead of our three colleagues travelling behind us.

Surprise Beach isn't a sandy beach. It's a promontory of steep cliffs covered with trees and bushes whipped by the wind. If you replaced the eucalyptus trees with gnarled pines and swapped the layer of thin grey-brown leaves for a mat of copper-coloured needles, this place would be almost like the Åland coastline.

Waves smash against the rocks below us. The wind is fairly strong. The white crests of waves can be seen flashing out to sea.

I find a good place for the tent, sheltered from the wind by the bushes to the south. Beside us there are a couple of fallen tree trunks that we can sit on. It's already pretty late, so we divide up the work. I go and fetch water while she gets the tent ready for the night.

The brook is further down near the sands at the bottom of what looks like a set of stairs hewn into the rock face. It is a bit like South Cape Rivulet but much shallower and wider. I have to go a long way upstream before I find water that doesn't taste of salt. The channel is so shallow that I wouldn't be able to fill the Platypus without using the wombat bottle.

The bottle reminds me of her: small and more pretty than useful, then all of a sudden revealing qualities you've never seen before.

When I get back to the camp she's already taken out the pot, the cooker and the plates. She suggests making up some packet soup and adding a bit of pasta. It would make for a good, sturdy meal, almost a casserole. That sounds like a plan.

But the water won't boil. The wind gusting in from the sea blows the cooker's flame sideways and low. We've got nothing to protect it from the wind. I try a couple of *ad hoc* solutions, but the water's heating up painfully slowly. Eventually a wisp of steam starts emanates from under the lid.

She tears open the packet of soup and hands it to me. I mix the powder into the water. She's reading the instructions on the packet of pasta. In a mildly bewildered voice she says you should boil it for eight minutes.

Eight minutes!

I wrench the packet of orzo from her hand. Orzo pasta is the size of a grain of rice; it should be cooked in just a few minutes. That's why I chose it in the first place: the same weight will fit into a smaller space than any other kind of pasta.

Eight minutes.

She might have read that in the supermarket seeing as she likes reading so bloody much.

If we start cooking the pasta in this sort of wind we'll have run out of gas before reaching Melaleuca. Of course we could just tip it into the boiling soup and turn off the heat, then keep it stewing under the lid. We could wrap the pot inside the sleeping-bag or something. It will cook, given time. I've no idea how long it would take, though.

The sky is already a dark evening blue. Night is closing in all around us, and she's got an imploring look in her eyes. We shouldn't mess around with the food any more than strictly necessary.

I suggest we leave out the pasta. Let's have the soup as soup. We can cut some meat from the length of salami. Then a couple of apricots for dessert.

She is quiet for a moment, then nods towards a pile of blackened stones. 'Couldn't we build a fire,' she asks, 'a real fire that we could cook on?'

Right. According to the guidebook, this camp and tomorrow's at Deadman's Bay are the only camps in Southy where you're allowed to build an open fire at the designated spot.

Then, thrilled at her own powers of observation, she says there should be loads and loads of good dry twigs in the bushes over there.

HEIDI

Jyrki runs his hand up and down the trunk of the nearest eucalyptus tree, then scuffs his boot through the thick layer of dried leaves on the ground.

'Look at that. What'll happen if even the smallest spark flies into that?

What'll happen in wind like this? And what happens when it spreads to the bush where, as we know, there are loads and loads of good dry twigs?'

The eucalyptus bark, or whatever it should be called, is like sheets of the finest silk paper, layer upon layer. Transparent silvery strips fluttering in the wind, as thin as a breath of air.

'These trees are so keen to be burnt that they grow their own kindling.'

Looking at them now, it is startlingly clear. Jyrki continues with something approaching admiration in his voice.

'These trees are full of flammable sap. Beneath this flaky tinder there's a thick layer of bark protecting the tree growing inside. The eucalyptus is a predator plant, a killer plant. It has adapted to fire, so much so that every now and then it needs to be burnt in order to germinate. But, at the same time, its own flammability makes it a kind of suicide bomber. It's clearing room for itself. When the forest burns down, the eucalyptus – and only the eucalyptus – will grow back again, with no competition whatsoever.'

. . . you thought yourself bewitched and cut off for ever from everything you had known once —
somewhere — far away — in another existence perhaps.

— Joseph Conrad, *Heart of Darkness*

NEW ZEALAND
Queen Charlotte Track
February 2007

JYRKI

Queen Charlotte Track was day-tourist material. To reach the start of the trail at Ship Cove, the bay where James Cook first set foot on this land, all you needed to do was take a water taxi from Picton. After a leisurely fifteen-kilometre stroll, if you wanted you could take another boat back to Picton from Forneaux Lodge.

In places this path was so well groomed that you'd have been fine if the sum total of your equipment was a pair of high heels. The route was cut to follow the ridges between two large fjords and to dip back and forth between miniature passes. The best thing was watching her expression every time a really breath-taking view opened up around another bend in the ridge.

We had reached Forneaux Lodge by four in the afternoon. Because we hadn't booked any accommodation, there was no point staying there. Punga Cove at Camp Bay was a four-hour hike away. It was on the opposite shore from Endeavour Inlet, so close you could almost see it. Having said that, the journey along the coastline would take almost as long as what we'd already done today.

There was no point having a big debate about it, because it was clear she had no idea of her own stamina. I felt almost claustrophobic at the thought of a long afternoon slouching around doing nothing in a bungalow hotel where, after having a shower, there'd be nothing else to do except hang around in the bar and wait for dinner.

We each munched a handful of mixed nuts and set off.

Towards the end the path became narrow and muddy. We had a tent, a cooker, a water filter and food, so in theory we could have spent the night almost anywhere. But at the beginning of our trip, and travelling with a novice, it was probably best to aim for some form of indoor accommodation.

She was pretty quiet on the final stretch towards Punga Cove. Twenty-seven kilometres. Not a bad initiation for a first-timer with a full pack on her back.

HEIDI

The longer the evening went on, the deeper my rucksack dug into my shoulders.

My feet ached.

Why can't we just stop while it still feels good, I remember muttering to myself – not out loud, though, as Jyrki was striding onwards in long bounding steps, mud splashing up around his shins and caking the tops of his hiking socks.

It was already eight o'clock by the time we arrived at Punga Cove. The reception desk was closed – in remote places like this I doubt people turn up out of the blue at this time of night.

We went into the restaurant, where we were told that there was room at the inn after all but that we couldn't get into our room until the shift manager turned up. Somebody called the shift manager. We learnt that the hotel's restaurant would be closing in half an hour but that the hotel complex had a communal kitchen where guests could cook their own food. We were already sweaty and muddy and exhausted, and now we were going to have to make do with a bowl of packet soup? But eventually the manager turned up and apologetically started checking the reservation book.

The only room available in the main building was a luxury suite of some sort. The rooms in another building a couple of hundred metres away were slightly cheaper, although the price difference was minimal.

I looked at Jyrki. His expression gave nothing away.

'I'll pay.' I took out my traveller's cheques. Jyrki had paid the backpackers' hostel in Picton on his credit card, so this was only fair. I had quite a wad of traveller's cheques; they should last a good while. I'd found someone to sublet my flat on the quiet, and she'd agreed to pay six months' rent up front if she could live there significantly cheaper than the going rate. Still, I knew this money wouldn't go far. The rent money had only just covered my flights, and the cost of Jyrki's list of expensive top-of-the-range hiking equipment that I was supposed to buy was enough to make your eyes water. His guiding principle was that if you bought something of the highest quality – which, of course, meant something expensive – it should be virtually indestructible.

As we filled in our room card, the waiter informed us that if we wanted to eat in the restaurant we'd have to order within the next twenty minutes.

We were back there in ten.

As we showered – to save time we showered together – and set a new world record for changing into fresh clothes, I was kicking myself because Punga Cove was so *nice*. Swimming pools, poolside bars, an obviously gourmet-standard restaurant, a room the size of a suite with its own door out on to a large private terrace shaded by a grove of palm trees and equipped with rattan furniture – all this and we only had one stupid night to enjoy it.

The issue of money came to mind again as I pulled my new, dizzyingly expensive, ultra-light but very warm Capilene shirt – which I had bought at Jyrki's suggestion – over my damp skin.

I was in the PR business after all; I was well aware of the power that came with reputation and information.

In the end it hadn't been all that difficult to get Antti-Pekka, the mid-level boss of the oil company, into a situation towards the end of a shared sauna evening in which he, after responding to my copious hints, went a bit too far with his chubby, greedy paws. I had been right in imagining that a drunken boss, thinking he was about to get lucky, would forget even the most elementary rules of caution. And it was no accident either that the changing-room we'd slunk away to was precisely the one in which Riitta had left her handbag, and I knew she couldn't survive for more than fifteen minutes without it. And so I got an eyewitness, and one from whose perspective the incident was clear cut.

I sobbed and trembled and talked about attempted rape, but when Riitta suggested I should press charges I seamlessly began talking about sexual harassment and indicated in a roundabout way that, as a developing professional in the field, I knew all too well that this wouldn't do the octane boys' public image any favours whatsoever. However, harassment was such a serious crime against humanity in general – and women in particular – that it would be wrong, *so* wrong, to hush it up.

Erkki shouted, Riitta anxiously tried to be understanding, Antti-Pekka was justifiably ice-cold and sarcastic, and it didn't take long for the oil sheikhs to dig ten thousands euros out of their bottomless pockets.

But at least I hadn't had to cause Dad the disappointment of resigning from the job he'd done so much to set up. After this little incident, the oil company said it couldn't foresee continued cooperation with our PR company and neither could the PR company with me.

For a moment I wondered whether I could have appealed against my dismissal, but that might have created too much of a situation.

I didn't answer any of Dad's telephone calls. I didn't answer when the doorbell rang.

He must have heard. And perhaps now he realized I could get by, using all of my own finest assets, in the hard-edged world of business.

But once we got to the restaurant and I had ordered my first bottle of lemon-flavoured Monteith's Radler, a lager that soon became the *vin ordinaire* of our New Zealand trip, lamb and roast vegetables with salad and parmesan risotto, I looked at Jyrki across the table (and, yes, at the end of the table there was a candle, and the panorama of fiords behind the window had turned a dark blue), and my heart melted like butter and sank down into my stomach.

Jyrki's eyes were locked on mine.

He reached his large angular hand across the table and placed it over the back of mine, and I felt almost dizzy.

'It'll soon be time to hit the sack.'

The words said one thing and his eyes another.

The mixture of lust and endorphin-induced euphoria brimmed and bubbled inside me so much that my hand was quivering beneath his, and I sensed that he could sense it.

You can fit a decent-sized one in your jacket pocket. Something bigger than a fist will make a nice dent when it hits the roof or the boot lid. The best is when it falls straight on the windscreen or bounces off the bonnet and back against the windscreen. Ante says he got a bounce once, and the car swerved into the lane of oncoming traffic and the brakes on the bus screeched as it tried to avoid the car, but there wasn't nothing about it in the paper.

There they are, in a line down below. Like quick, scurrying beetles.

Ante says they never put this sort of thing in the paper. Like they don't run stories about people that jump off observation towers. You'd just get more people wanting to have a go.

He says he saw the what-the-fuck look on the driver's face as the glass shattered in front of him. I doubt it. You can't see people's expressions at that height or speed. Then there's all them shards in the way and all.

SOUTH COAST TRACK, TASMANIA
Surprise Bay
Tuesday, March 2007

JYRKI

I wake up to find her prodding me. Her nervous whisper cuts the sticky air like a saw.

It's impenetrably dark. The rush of the waves forms a thick sonic backdrop to the night.

Then I hear it, too.

A thud. A thump, the sound of something being dragged, then another thump. Something is moving the dishes in the vestibule of the tent.

We haven't bothered washing them up, just wiped them with a scrap of tissue paper. They are probably still giving off the strong smell of pumpkin soup. The bag of food is in my rucksack, tied securely behind an array of clips and drawstrings. Nothing should be able to get into that.

I undo the zip on the sleeping-bag. The sounds stop immediately. Someone or something freezes on the spot and listens.

The night air is biting. I reach my hand into the corner pocket inside the tent. The headlamp case is right there. I kneel down and open the case. I fumble with it to make sure it's the right way round, then place it on my head and switch it on.

The brightness of the LED light feels almost like a slap in the face.

I open up the zips straight away, with both hands, at both sides, the mosquito net, the door.

The pot and the plates are no longer in the vestibule. One of the cups is lying on its side beside our boots and gas cylinder.

Still on my knees, I unzip the vestibule door and shine the beam of light emanating from my forehead out into the thick Tasmanian night. I let out a frightening shout, allowing a mixture of roaring and bellowing to pour out of my throat.

I hear two frenzied rustling sounds, then swooshing, pattering. Footsteps, paws, a tail — or what?

Another snap, further off. Then silence.

The roar of the waves mixes with the rush of blood in my ears.

I crawl outside and stand upright. The LED cuts a slice out of the darkness, leaving everything outside its beam utterly impenetrable. I switch it off. After a moment I begin to make out the swaying boughs of the trees against the slightly lighter sky. I see a couple of stars between the frenzied churning clouds. A dim glow can be seen behind the trees; the moon has risen but is hidden behind the clouds.

I see a lighter patch on the ground. The plastic bag with the dishes. The pot hadn't been dragged very far; it must have been too heavy. I flick the headlamp back on. Yes, the other cup and both plates are lying on the ground, one of them upside down. I pick up the dishes and put them back in the plastic bag. At least our multipurpose spoon-cum-forks are still at the bottom of the bag.

The beam of light shines in her face as I crawl back into the tent. She turns away, squinting, and raises her hand up to cover her face. I throw the bag of dishes into the corner.

'Some possum must have taken too many steroids,' I tell her.

And this stillness of life did not in the least resemble a peace. It was the stillness of an implacable force brooding over an inscrutable intention. It looked at you with a vengeful aspect.

– Joseph Conrad, *Heart of Darkness*

HEIDI

The subtropical forest at the start of Kepler Track was something incredible. It was full of twittering, buzzing and the cheeping of birds. It wouldn't have taken long to come up with several dozen chirpy new ringtones.

Every now and then, great panoramas looking out towards Lake Te Anau opened up through the trees, all the more awe-inspiring the higher we climbed, and it was then that I began to understand Jyrki properly. Hiking itself isn't the prize; this is the prize, these views that you can look at from places you can reach only on foot.

Rain started falling in a thin drizzle, and we stopped at the resting place to change our clothes. A brown bird the size of a chicken came over straight away to greet us. It didn't seem at all scared. Jyrki told me it was a weka, the New Zealand equivalent of the Siberian jay. It was a very social bird that waited for hikers to drop something nice to eat. I broke it off a few morsels of puffed rice from the top of my energy bar.

JYRKI

I had said my quiet goodbyes to hotels, hostels, restaurants and tiled bath-rooms.

Back at Queen Charlotte you would have no trouble finding some sort of accommodation for the night. And after thirty sweaty kilometres what was wrong with being able to have a shower then retire to the terrace restaurant for a bowl of fruits-de-mer soup and some garlic bread? Now at Kepler it was time to move on to some tougher challenges. Or so I thought.

I chose Kepler Track on the South Island, one of the so-called Great Walks. It was great for a number of reasons.

For a start, according to the guidebooks it wasn't as outrageously popular as Milford or Abel Tasman. You could ramble along Kepler Track without booking monthsin advance, although needless to say we had done so anyway. What's more, you could reach the start of the track from the town of Te Anau on foot — after all, what was the point of hiking if you had to rent a car or take a taxi to get you to the start of the track?

In addition, Te Anau seemed like a much smaller, more pleasant base for our hike than places like Queenstown which were crammed with tourists.

At Te Anau we took care of our registration. We were given hut tickets and were told that they were binding: you had to spend the night in the cabins you had reserved. No improvisation. Not because of the weather, not for health reasons, under no circumstances whatsoever. Arrive at the wrong cabin at the wrong time and you'd get slapped with a fine on the spot.

It makes the mind boggle.

It was less than an hour's walk from Te Anau to the start of Kepler Track. I almost burst out laughing when I heard that there was — wait for it — a *shuttle service* from the town to the start of the track. A few poxy kilometres. Taking a minibus just to be able to walk.

According to the instruction leaflets, the first leg should take about six hours. By half past one we'd seen a sign saying it was another forty-five minutes' walk to the Luxmoor cabin.

I almost lost my temper. We'd completed the leg in about half the estimated time, yet we had no choice but to stop here for the night. Given that these cabins cost the same as a fairly decent hotel, you would think we would at least be given the chance to choose our own prison.

Still, a thousand metres above sea level, when the drizzle started to turn to sleet, the idea of being able to shelter under a proper roof didn't feel so bad, but when I saw the cabin from the inside the urge to yell welled up yet again.

The place was filled with kitchen surfaces holding dozens of gas hobs. Just turn the knob and start cooking. There was a shower and an indoor toilet.

A coal fireplace.

If it hadn't been sleeting outside, and if all this hadn't already been paid for, I would have turned around and walked right back to Te Anau.

Conveniences like this are only convenient if you actually want them.

Inside the cabin an Israeli guy was boiling up some pasta. Of all the equipment in the world, this first-rate amateur was carrying a three-litre aluminium pot, the kind you use in your own kitchen. And he was wearing a long-sleeved white cotton shirt.

The most impractical colour and fabric you could possibly imagine. Once it gets wet it loses any advantageous qualities it ever had. The shirt would take a lifetime to dry.

What were these people *doing*? Or what did they *think* they were doing?

It's usually baked beans or fish fingers or yoghurt or something like that. Sometimes there's a slice of some fancy ham or a jar of something that's obviously cost a bit. A length of liver sausage or something else soft can do the trick in the toilets in a department store or café, or you can drop an egg down a hole, somewhere it's impossible to get it out, and hope it cracks. But mostly I just look at 'em. Imagining what they would've done with this or that food.

People are always turning their backs on their shopping bags. When they're packing another bag or waiting for the bus or looking through the bus window waiting to get off.

Five fingers and Bob's your uncle.

If there's a driver's licence or some other photo ID in the wallet, I check to see what someone that buys tinned pineapple or granary toast actually looks like. What kind of kids they've got. Gormless idiots mostly. And I take the money, too.

If there's something halfway decent in the bags, like cake or chocolate, I might even eat it.

Once I found a pair of expensive leather gloves; they'd just been bought, receipt still attached and everything. Too small for me, and I could've swapped them with that receipt for ones that fitted better. But if I need leather gloves, I tell the old man my hands are cold, and before you know it I've got three pairs, and one of them'll probably have fucking mink lining.

You need to call him Dad. Works every time. Just start off with 'Hi Dad.' Honest, that word's like magic; it's hard not to laugh when you see it in action. After that it's easy to tell him that such-and-such a policeman was a sadistic fucker, or the woman in the shop was a paranoid menopausal bitch. You need to look at him with your head tilted a bit to the side, with the left eye slightly forwards. Don't smile too much, or he'll say there's nothing funny about it. Then again, if you're too serious he'll think you're worried or afraid. When he's having a rant, you need to look at his lips and sometimes his eyes and nod and try to kill time.

I left the whole fucking lot in the foyer at the cinema.

Kenu always tries to leave the bags at the station or in the bank or some place where people notice an unattended bag pronto. Said he'd once watched from the sidelines while a police bomb squad crawled up to a black leather bag with pincers in their hands, only to find nothing but a sack of potatoes and a porno mag.

TASMANIA
Surprise Bay to Deadman's Bay
Wednesday, March 2007

HEIDI

A few hours after leaving Surprise Bay we come to a fork in the road leading to Osmiridium Beach.

'Some idiots try to divide the leg in two by spending the night over there,' Jyrki says, pointing his hiking pole down towards the beach. The spot is almost an hour's walk away.

Although I can hardly deny that this would be enough for one day, thank you very much, I realize that setting up camp and killing the hours until it's time to go to bed would bore us both to death. It feels almost macho to continue on our way without giving the matter a second thought.

Naturally everyone who embarks on one of these hikes has to bid farewell to all normal ways of keeping themselves entertained. Of course you can't *force* an adult to give up their mp3 player, a gadget that weighs only a few grams, but the chuckle of disdain that Jyrki can give in just the right way when he sees something he doesn't approve of is enough to make you think twice.

Though the beach extends as far as the eye can see, swimming isn't recommended here because there are very strong currents in the water. That said, I wouldn't want to go swimming if I couldn't have a fresh-water shower afterwards. Anyone who's ever swum at the seaside and got dressed without a shower knows what it means to feel stickier than sticky; your hair feels as though you've used syrup instead of conditioner.

It's occurred to me here for the first time that, more often than not, people tend to eat and drink simply as a way of passing time. We have a coffee and a slice of cake because there's nothing else to do. We sit having a beer. We go for a kebab. Out here, in these conditions, you eat to give yourself energy, and there's absolutely nothing extra to nibble on.

Ergo, there is *nothing* to do.

Back in New Zealand I still carried a book with me. Almost every backpackers' hostel had a bookshelf where people could leave the books they'd read and pick up something new. I chose the smallest and thinnest paperback I could find: Joseph Conrad's *Heart of Darkness*. I enjoy reading, but I didn't know anything about this book. It sounded promisingly like a horror story. It wasn't. Or rather, yes, it was.

I read it four times. Maybe five.

But now I have nothing to read. There's no room for being a hero when it comes to the weight of your rucksack, or so I've heard. The best way to kill time is simply to march onwards, especially while the terrain is bearable. When we cross a pair of logs across Tyler's Creek, the stream from which people collect drinking water once they get down to Osmiridium Beach, Jyrki stops to examine the water.

The creek is shallow and the water is far browner than I've become used to; it's muddy, almost dried up.

'It's a good job we didn't go down to Osmiridium. We'd have had to filter all the water. Must be unusually dry around here at the moment,' Jyrki comments, poking his hiking pole into the creek.

'Where did they come up with a name like that? It sounds like something out of a bad sci-fi novel.'

'It's a real word. It's a metal related to platinum, a compound of osmium and iridium if I remember right. Maybe people have mined it around here; there's been tin mining in Melaleuca, too.'

'What can you make out of it? Rings?'

'Small things that are put under hard sustained pressure.'

'Such as?'

I smile wryly at my question; I only spot the *double entendre* after I've said it. Now would be the time for a light-hearted compliment.

Jyrki's face lights up; you can see the light bulb switching on in his head. I wait patiently.

'The nib of a fountain pen,' he says.

JYRKI

The location of the creek's outlet is constantly moving. The exact spot where it decides to burst a sandbank can shift by a couple of kilometres at a time. Sometimes there are two outlets at once. The shallower one, the one that sometimes almost disappears, is one we should be able to wade across easily.

The map gives us a choice of routes. I go for the one running adjacent to the sandbank.

Of course, there's no path on the sandbank, just some tufts of grass and a dune whipped up by the wind. Perhaps that row of marks, like melted dents in the ground, could be the prints from yesterday's hiking boots.

My feet sink into the sand, and in no time so much sand has come in through the top of my boots that I can't move my feet inside them at all; it feels as though they've been set in a plaster cast. My boots are like dead weights. I can only guess at the route. I know the general direction, of course, but where exactly are we supposed to cross the shallow river outlet? I try to look for signs along the steep embankment on the other side, anything at all.

She asks how long this is going to take. I tell her we're nearly there.

To the left is the ocean, to the right the brown, deep and rapid-flowing New River Lagoon outlet and behind that an embankment reaching up towards the sky. We stagger along the bank like two insects in a sandpit. Although by now there should be weeks of routine in my thigh muscles, in this loose sand I have to lift my legs like a stiff arthritic mutt.

Then I see something further up the embankment. It's almost like a set of steps up the hillside; a few horizontal logs and something that looks like iron chains glinting beneath the sand. I stand there catching my breath. My face and neck are covered in fine sand carried on the wind and stuck to my sweat. I am the sandman, from head to toe.

But before we can reach what apparently passes for a path we first have to cross the second outlet from the lagoon. The water comes up to just above the knee – a welcome reason to take off our boots and empty half a kilo of crap out of each one.

Once we reach the other side it will be impossible to put socks on our wet feet without getting them caked with sand. Must remember to turn them inside out later on and give them a shake. If we don't, they'll chafe like sandpaper.

The weight of the rucksack pulls me backwards as we scale the almost vertical embankment. Time and time again we have to grab on to the iron chains and whip more sand up into our faces. Some of the logs laid down to form steps have come away from the pegs keeping them in place. Behind some of them, the sand has flowed away or been scattered by the wind so much that the logs are like shelves wobbling in the air.

She's huffing and puffing her way up the embankment in front of me.

Every time her foot slips another cloud of sand billows into my face. I shout up to her to keep a safe distance. If she falls and I'm too close behind her, then we'll both be screwed. She turns to look down at me and says that I'm the one that should keep a safe distance by not coming up so fast.

HEIDI

An aluminium dinghy has been pulled far up on to the shore, for understandable reasons, and tied to a wooden pole with a rope and a couple of carabiners. The oars have been propped upright in a piece of plastic piping nailed to the side of the pole.

On the opposite shore, about a hundred metres away, there appears to be another boat and a colourful buoy raised on a pole.

On this side, too, there is a signpost and a board with instructions. The instructions are also given in pictures – probably for us foreigners and all the crowds of illiterate people that surely swarm here every day. Working out the boat system is like doing a minor Mensa puzzle: first you take this boat, row to the opposite shore and leave all your stuff. Then you take the other boat, tie it to the back of the first boat and row back with both of them. Pull one of the dinghies far up on to the shore and tie it down securely, then row back to the opposite shore with the other boat and tie it up ready for the next customers.

I wonder how many people have thought: Screw this. Anyone could cross the river and just leave both boats on the other side. Arriving here and seeing both dinghies on the opposite shore would be a sight you wouldn't forget for a while. And if you were the lucky person this happened to, you'd have plenty of time to sit there meditating, waiting for some unlikely Godot to show up on the opposite shore.

The dinghy is bloody heavy. By myself I might just have been able to push it into the water, but I could never have hauled it far enough up the soft sands of the opposite shore as it needed to be.

If I were here by myself, I might have taken the easy way out, too. Dragging that dinghy across the sand would be hard work for an athletic man, let alone a woman. I would row across and leave both boats on the same shore. Hadn't Jyrki said something about most hikers going the other way around Southy? So, statistically speaking, someone was more likely to turn up at the shore with two boats first. I'd be doing someone a favour.

Once the dinghy is in the water, Jyrki climbs in and puts the oars in the rowlocks.

I know what to do next: I push the boat with both hands, at a run, and hop on to the thwart seat so that the speed and my added weight gently carry it far out into the current.

Jyrki puts the oars into the water. He pulls, and one of the oars sinks deep beneath the water leaving the other to skim the surface. Jyrki gives a heave; his second attempt isn't much better either.

Jyrki can't row.

The idea seems a bit baffling, and the longer I watch him the more comical his flailing becomes, especially when one's desperately trying to keep a straight face.

The boat lolls from side to side, the bow pointing first one way then another. Every time he tries to row, one of the oars sinks in deeper than the other. Eventually we reach the opposite shore almost sideways. Once we've unloaded our rucksacks, untethered the other boat and tied it to the back of ours I take hold of the oars.

'How about I give it a go?'

Jyrki doesn't say a word. I sit on the middle thwart and let Jyrki push the boat out into the water. He almost capsizes the thing trying to imitate me as, scrambling and splashing, he comes crashing down on the back thwart.

I keep both oars at the same height and row in clear, even strokes. At least I've learnt something at our family's summer cottage: the bow touches down on the other shore before I've even really got started. Using our push-and-pull technique, we return the other boat to its own pole. Hauling it up the slight incline is almost impossible. The push and pull have to happen at precisely the same fraction of a second, otherwise the boat won't move an inch.

Jyrki lets me take the oars without any further discussion. Who would have thought it?

It's been almost two hours since we first arrived at the outlet when I finally sit down on the edge of the boat, fastened securely to its pole, and start to pull on my socks and boots. Jyrki shakes his head.

'We've got four kilometres of sandy beaches ahead. I wouldn't bother with those.'

JYRKI

The sandy beach: synonymous with that shiny jungle of parasols and Speedo kings sunning themselves in the heat; in the background, the incessant thump of pop music from the terrace bars of giant hotels scraping the sky. Along the beach, rows of identikit overpriced caffs all out to maximize their profits. Isn't that right?

Prion Beach is an exception to the laws of nature; it's as though a neutron bomb had exploded. How come there isn't a single sun-worshipper on this four-kilometre crescent of white sandy shores washed by foaming waves? Not a single flip-flop print; not a can of beer half buried in the sand; not a cigarette end. How could anyone have overseen such a clear gap in the market? Why had nobody thought to construct a Hobart to Melaleuca motorway so that people could nip out to this glinting golden paradise without a care in the world?

As if in answer to my question I hear a familiar buzzing high up above us: the daily small aircraft travelling back and forth to Melaleuca. Its dung-fly droning always finds its way into your ears just as you've finally accepted your oneness with the wilderness, just as you're about to sever the final thinning ties between yourself and civilization.

On my hiking trips around Europe, even in the most remote Alpine regions of Switzerland, Italy or France, you took it for granted that the sky would be laced with the trails of jet engines or that helicopters would chatter overhead at regular intervals, carrying out a variety of maintenance operations in remote mountain villages. But out here there are no vapour trails twining like ropes criss-crossing the sky. Out here the sky shouldn't be corseted like that.

Once we get past Melaleuca and reach Old Port Davey Track we won't have to see or hear any flying machines. There you can breathe the air of freedom.

His need was to exist, and to move onwards at the greatest possible risk, and with a maximum of privation. If the absolutely pure, uncalculating, unpractical spirit of adventure had ever ruled a human being, it ruled this be-patched youth.

— Joseph Conrad, *Heart of Darkness*

HEIDI

To pass the time that afternoon we boiled up a beef stock cube and sipped it from mugs with some pieces of bread. We chatted to a German guy who had spent the summer in Eastern Finland a few years ago and still raved about the quality of the light and the hush of the pine trees.

The cabin at Luxmoor was surrounded by a wooden terrace from which you could gaze down at the stunning panorama of fiord-like lakes whenever the misty, rainy weather deigned to draw back its curtains for a moment.

A bird fluttered down and landed on the terrace railing.

It was a gleaming emerald-grey colour and had a hooked beak and large claws. At the base of its beak its nostrils rose up in a ragged yellow lump. It watched us steadily, not the least bit scared.

I remembered the inquisitive, cute little weka. I put my mug on the railing and, using my fingers, ripped off a piece of the bread roll I had bought in Te Anau and gingerly placed it on the railing. The bird looked at it, then looked at me – almost shamelessly, you might say – and took a step closer to the chunk of bread with its large, nimble, sharp-clawed feet.

Just then a hand swept across the railing and snatched the piece of bread, crushed it in a fist and handed it – no, shoved it – back to me.

'Don't do that. Ever again,' said the man.

I could feel my face turning red.

'What's the matter?' I managed to splutter.

'That's a kea.'

Kii-a. I realized straight away that the bird had been named after its own call.

The man was a ranger, a park keeper who lived at Luxmoor during the peak season. 'When these birds eat too many processed carbohydrates from the tourists they don't have any inclination to look for their own food. Then they come up with alternative pastimes.'

I looked at Jyrki. For him there was no insult worse than being called a tourist. His nostrils flared, and with his sharp nose for a moment he looked almost like the kea itself.

The ranger told us that keas only live at altitudes of a thousand metres and above. And that they're smart and nasty as anything.

As the bike sinks beneath the water in the harbour and the last thing you see is its white saddle, things start popping into my mind.

Ante always says you can tell what kind of person last rode a bike by sniffing the saddle.

But nothing can keep its scent for ever, like you can't take a foreign country home with you. Nobody can walk around for the rest of their lives with the smell from, like, Australia hanging around them, so people can see straight away they've been somewhere. They've always got to bring it up themselves and bore other people with their fucking holiday photos.

People think that if they do something they believe is real, even if they don't enjoy doing it one bit, they'll be fighting off medals and awards when they get home.

And what about when they've kicked the bucket? At least they'll end up with a bit of decent company: a stone that's as dead as stones can be and a layer of flowers that are even deader.

There's another bike in range. There's no one about, only a couple of pissheads getting into a scrap a bit further off, and their field of vision extends only as far as the spit flying from their mouths.

A few steps and the wheel's off the bike stand. If it had been locked with a chain they'd both have gone. Bike stands are a good weight. If you lift it by the carrier at the back, it's easy to push the locked bike a couple of metres using only the front wheel. Splashety splash.

And now nobody will ever sniff it again.

Where once something stood, now there's nothing but an empty space and the harbour is a little bit fuller. Something in the world has moved, and later on it'll snowball. Maybe tomorrow when someone turns up and says to themselves, I'm sure I left it here.

HEIDI

Any beach can be wonderful, amazing and marvellous when you walk along it for four hundred metres.

But a beach can be a total fucking nightmare when you walk along it for four kilometres.

Normally you'd stroll along the shore and enjoy digging your toes into the sand. Normally it would feel nice when your foot sinks into the dunes.

Normally you wouldn't have a twelve-kilo rucksack on your shoulders and hiking boots dangling around your neck, their heels and toes constantly pummelling against your ribs.

Normally it would feel wonderful to let the sea breeze flutter through your hair.

Normally you would actually have hair.

In other places you would walk slowly, enjoying the smell of salt in the air, admiring the magnificent waves and foaming crests. Here you plod onwards, dripping in sweat, only to realize after half an hour that you can't see a thing. Or that you can see but only through a strange, blurred fog. And then you notice that the watery mist, whipped up from the sea by the wind and with a good dose of salt, collects on the surface of your sunglasses so that everything looks dim and obscured, every bit as annoying as a piece of apple skin stuck stubbornly between your teeth – you can't forget about it, and you can't think about anything else.

When I try to start cleaning my sunglasses I see that I only have a few tissues left in a packet crumpled up in the pocket of my shorts. Jyrki has another packet, although I've no idea how many are left. It might even be empty.

I feel a chill run through me as I remember that we didn't buy any more. Everything else but not tissues. Jyrki assumed complete authority over our shopping trip at the Woolworth's in Hobart, so how the hell have we ended up without any *tissues*? You need them all the time: for scrubbing dishes, to use as toilet paper, to clean cuts and scratches and for all kinds of basic cleaning. Such as scraping the salty crud off the lenses of your sunglasses, because no matter what else I try and use – the hem of my T-shirt, the edge of my shorts, in desperation I even dig a shirt sleeve out of the bag of camp clothes in my rucksack – every piece of fabric I have with me is soaked in just enough sweat or sun-cream or some other shite that my glasses simply will not clean. Although they might get a bit brighter they're still coated in an annoying film that refracts the light at will, leaving me almost half blind.

Once we set up camp maybe I'll try using the cotton lining of my only pair of clean underpants, but until then I have to look at this awe-inspiring landscape as though a thin blurry gauze had been drawn between it and me, making the view seem dull and giving me a headache into the bargain.

At the western end of the shore, where we are supposed to start climbing back into the woods, is a stream running across the sand. By the side of the stream is a pole with a sign and a couple of giant plastic vegetable scrubbers hanging on a peg.

'I see. Time for a wash.'

The sign bears a word that I don't recognize: phytophthora.

'The Europeans must have brought it here,' says Jyrki, already kneeling by the water's edge with a boot in one hand and a scrubber in the other. 'Root rot. It's some sort of fungus that kills local plants. At the moment it's one of the most destructive plant diseases in the world; it threatens something like nine hundred species here alone. And that, of course, threatens animals as they lose their food and shelter. It spreads through mud and soil, so via car tyres and shoes, that sort of thing. We must be about to enter an uninfected area.'

Right. A *biohazard*. We were both examined at the customs office in Auckland when we first arrived in New Zealand. We had to declare our tent, boots, hiking poles, the works. My equipment was brand new, but Jyrki's stuff was checked and disinfected, meaning that we almost missed our connecting flight to Wellington.

I turn my boots in my hands. They are crusted in a thick layer of mud, and the idea of trying to scrape them clean seems absolutely hopeless. Why did I have to choose the ones with the nubuck surface, just because they looked cool?

'Is it really that important?'

Jyrki jumps to his feet, muddy water splashing around him, and looks at me as though I'd just suggested barbecuing a baby.

'Yes, it is!'

The layer of dried mud seems like it'll never come off the boots, although the brushes have stiff bristles. We crouch there in silence; the swishing of the scrubbers reminds me of washing rugs by the lake, and for a moment I am in Finland again where summer is so familiar: the birch trees and the rowan, the lapping of the lake, the song thrush and the chaffinch. The silent dusk of a summer's night, the dull applause of the aspen leaves, and . . .

Then I can hear those old lyrics so clearly that I can feel my throat tightening: *How lonely is your shore, and how I yearn for there* . . .

When I finally open my eyes and see the untamed swells of the Southern Ocean I feel such a wave of angst that I have to catch my breath. People would give their left arm to get to experience a place like this, and still I yearn to be somewhere else.

And yet there was probably never a shore quite as lonely as this one.

I look up at Jyrki. He has already finished cleaning his boots and has started scouring the tent hooks.

JYRKI

There are active crimes, and then there are passive crimes.

A passive crime is the act of not doing something.

A fledgeling first-timer hiker, your bog-standard Aussie, stepping on this unknown virgin soil as a conqueror just like his ancestors, would look at that sign, those brushes, and scoff. In the self-appointed sacred name of individual freedom his shoes would remain firmly on his feet. People can decide for themselves how to spend their time; it's Everyman's Right – particularly when nobody is there to check on you.

Nobody was watching back when the Europeans arrived in Australia and the axes started flying. Indigenous tribes were ravaged first by disease, then deportation and, finally, through a systematic child-removal policy. The rich soil was robbed, leaving nothing but a barren salt desert. The government even paid blood money for the destruction of natural vegetation: a hefty tax cut for every cleared hectare. And so farmers tied a heavy iron chain between two tractors and drove them side by side. Regardless of whether the area was ever to be cultivated or not, the chains ripped all indigenous plants up from the ground by the roots. The land was effectively shaved bald. Nature itself became the victim of genocide.

It made me think of Finland in the 1960s, when the state financed the clearing of land while simultaneously paying farmers to leave their fields fallow.

The Europeans who first arrived in Australia seemed to think that, because the island's latitudinal location and its climate somewhat resembled those at home, the land must automatically have all the necessary preconditions for extensive crop-growing and cattle-rearing. And because the island was partially covered with giant forests, tall enough to rival the sequoias of California, people assumed that beneath them must be a layer of fertile humus. But what they didn't know was that the majority of the nutrients in this ancient terrain were in the plants themselves and not in the soil.

Settlers arrived in the spirit of freedom and happiness with the flag of enterprise flying high. And, almost in passing, they ransacked an entire continent and brought it to within an inch of its life.

At first this island was a penal colony.

A man arrived in Australia, and the immigration official asked him if he had a criminal record. The man replied that he didn't know it was still an entry requirement.

Out here a farmer — who if he's lucky might have a farm the size of Wales — deliberately burns down the forest so that a few weeks later his sheep can eat spear grass, the juicy green shoots of the first plants to push their way through the ashes.

When people fell a palm tree — which otherwise might feed an entire village — so they can have palm shoots in their salad, when we kill a shark for its fins or shoot an elephant for its tusks, it's small beer compared with this. But there's no point getting on a high horse about it: in just the same way, protected forests along the Mediterranean coast are secretly set alight so that eventually there will be nothing left to protect. Then someone can snap up the land for next to nothing, build a couple of fifteen-star hotels and fill their restaurants with imported Sri Lankan tuna while a couple of metres away on the beach Giorgios's fishing business is suffocating in a sea full of plastic bags and tourists' diarrhoea.

We see two wallabies as we climb up the ridge from Prion into the forest. They take fright and dash into the thick bushes with a frantic rustling. I can imagine them desperately scrambling with the sheep for fresh grass on the black terrain, the kind that Bill described back at the Grampians.

We wipe our feet before stepping into someone's home, but we don't care what kind of dirt and destruction we spread across other creatures' territories.

In a few years the Tasmanian devil will probably become extinct. The species is plagued by a disease causing nasty growths around the head. The disease has spread to Tasmania only in the last ten years. Unlike phytophthora, it might not have been brought here by humans. But if the population continues to fall at this rate – and even if some individuals turn out to be immune and can continue the species – the foxes and cats that humans have introduced to the island will quickly find their way into the little devils' ecological niche. This is exactly what happened in New Zealand: the possums brought over from Australia destroyed, and continue to destroy, indigenous fauna so fast and effectively that you can almost hear the daily slaughter in the bushes.

Our forefathers committed active crimes in the name of their own happiness. The generations that followed have opted for passive crimes, for precisely the same reasons, and seem happy to stand by watching a chain of ethnic cleansing, both other people's and their own. There's nothing you can do about it; that's the way the world goes around; we have our rights. The way your average Yank talks about climate change: are we going to let a few polar bears threaten the American Way of Life?

And what about those polar bears and tigers? Yeah, well, at least one day they might bring in hordes of gawping tourists.

Once all the other fauna have been destroyed Australia could well see a surge in the popularity of fox-hunting, after the wise decision to ship in foxes to take care of the even more wisely shipped-in rabbits. Once devastated by phytophthora, the indigenous flora can be replaced by some nice imported plant species that the wallabies can't digest. Then we won't have to shoo them off the hotel gardens all the time.

To tear treasure out of the bowels of the land was their desire, with no more moral purpose at the back of it than there is in burglars breaking into a safe.

— Joseph Conrad, *Heart of Darkness*

NEW ZEALAND
Nelson Lakes
February 2007

JYRKI

At the lakes in Nelson the tracks were real tracks, not small minor roads. Across the rivers there were rope bridges, proper rickety ones that can only take one person at a time.

The silence was perfect.

If I'd been able to choose now, I would have come from Queen Charlotte straight out here to Nelson. It would have been a much shorter trip, too, but instead we'd gone and booked those bloody berths in Kepler.

At least here you had the freedom to decide for yourself how long each leg was going to take. We'd left St Arnaud in good time that morning, and our aim was to complete a 27-kilometre stretch of even terrain on a gentle incline before ending up at Upper Travers Hut. According to the guidebook, the leg should take somewhere between ten and eleven hours.

We hadn't encountered anyone else for the last few hours. Occasionally, when we came out of the forest cover, we were able to see Mount Travers. Its peak was covered in snow. At last, a fleeting glimpse of something real.

Having said that, Upper Travers Hut itself was big and new. Two separate dormitories; berths in bunk beds for about thirty people, each one equipped with a thick foam mattress covered in wax cloth. An enormous lounge with a kitchen area and dining tables and chairs. A veranda. A composting outdoor toilet a decent walk from the hut and a large tank to collect rainwater.

At least we were the only people in the hut.

Even out here they charged for the use of the cabins, all except for the most basic shacks. The price was in a different league to those along the Great Walks. The series of tickets cost only a couple of New Zealand dollars, and you were supposed to leave individual tickets in the cabins according to their standard. This cabin cost two tickets. Each ticket had a perforated tear-off section with the same serial number on the remaining stub. The idea was to keep one half of the ticket and leave it somewhere visible while you were staying at the hut — attaching it to the straps of your rucksack, for instance. The other half was to be dropped into a locked postbox on the wall of the cabin. If the ranger taking care of the track happened to come in and inspect the cabin, you could easily check to see who had paid. Freeloaders could expect a substantial fine.

I'd bought a book of eight tickets back in St Arnaud, but I should have bought sixteen. It was an oversight. Two times four nights, times two. I'd only counted enough for myself.

At least it was quiet now, and it would soon be dusk. Nobody would turn up after dark.

She'd thrown her rucksack on to the floor in one of the dormitories and was busy digging out her civvies. She'd just pulled her sports bra over her head and was groping for her sweat-free clothes when I moved my hand swiftly and stopped her in her tracks.

She looked at me, and the sports bra fell to the floor. Her beautiful breasts, the size of a fist, heaved slowly. The chilly air in the cabin and her damp clothes had left her nipples wrinkled like raisins.

I kissed her and said that now was the time.

HEIDI

Sex?

There I stood in nothing but my panties, my skin covered in goosebumps, ready to collapse into anything that was clean and dry; the sun was setting and the air getting colder, and here was Jyrki coming at me in this primitive shack halfway up a wooded mountainside when I was absolutely exhausted and wanted nothing but food and sleep.

'Time for a wash.'

'I don't know if I'm really in the mood for . . . A wash?'

'Naked. Bring your mug. And a towel.'

Jyrki was already rummaging through his own rucksack and soon produced the said items. I must have been looking at him like a madman as he started taking off his own clothes.

'Out by the back door there's a barrel of rainwater. There's no stream round here, so we'll have to use the water in the tank — but sparingly, mind.'

'But that'll be cold.'

'What were you expecting?'

Jyrki walked across the dormitory in all his naked glory and strode towards the emergency exit, a mug in one hand and a towel the size of a handkerchief that he'd bought in Wellington in the other: a super-absorbent travel towel packed in a small netted bag, the kind that, apparently, you couldn't get anywhere in Finland.

'We shouldn't bother with soap. You won't be able to rinse it off properly, and it'll just lie in the soil.'

The door was draughty. Although it was already cold inside the cabin, the sudden gust of chill air was a reminder of the not-so-distant Antarctic.

'Well?'

I followed Jyrki to the door. He had placed his opened towel on the railing and was now crouching down filling his mug with water from the tank. I almost shrieked as he poured the water over his head, scrubbed himself using his hands and repeated this with another mugful of water.

'Pouring it slowly like this, you can make a little bit of water go a long way. Gets the sweat off the skin. This is basic stuff. If you don't wash the film of sweat off your skin, you can bet you'll catch a chill at night.'

The shock had me speechless. Wasn't it part of the life of a macho hiker-man to be unashamedly dirty and smelly? I'd much rather be dirty and smelly and blokier than thou than pour cold water over myself at a time when my teeth were already chattering from the cold.

'Sometimes it's easier if someone else does it,' said Jyrki, and before I'd had time to say anything he had poured a mugful of water down the back of my neck.

I screamed so loudly that the sound echoed around the woods and the mountainside. It was as if a vat of molten metal had suddenly been tipped over me, but Jyrki continued unhurriedly pouring water over my back, sides and buttocks, scrubbing me with his big hands, and, as if by a miracle, I suddenly found myself in a Zen-like state of tranquillity. I stood there silently as he returned with another mugful, and together his hands and the water removed the sweat from my breasts, my stomach and thighs.

'Face,' said Jyrki and poured water into my cupped hands. I rinsed my face and felt beneath my fingers the coat of dried sweat across my forehead and around the sides of my jaws; it came away in my hands like a layer of fine sand.

'Now dry off,' he told me.

I didn't have a special travel towel, but I did have a thin cotton sarong. It was much larger and heavier, of course, but it had already been put to plenty of different uses, everything from a picnic tablecloth to an improvised dressing-gown in hostels with the shower in the corridor.

I wrapped the sarong around myself and towelled myself off, and suddenly everything seemed to make perfect sense. My toes and the area between my shoulder blades ached, but I wasn't cold any more, not one bit.

Just then something hit my arm so hard that it smarted. The impact was almost electric – sharp and painful. Another blow to my shoulders; a third on my forehead. And only then did I notice that a cloud of black dots had gathered around us.

'Damn it. Sand flies,' said Jyrki and swiped at the cloud of insects to make it disperse, opened the door as little as possible and pulled me inside. A few black dots followed us inside but thankfully not very many.

'We'll be able to swat them. From now on we need to be careful opening the door. Maybe we should go to the toilet via the lounge, so we don't need to open any doors directly outside.'

I nodded, sat down on the edge of a bunk and started pulling on dry, warm clothes. I felt so wonderful that I could have burst into tears.

JYRKI

There was a rattle from the veranda. I was setting up our cooker on the metal-plated work surface in the kitchen. I decided that if the newcomer was a ranger I'd say I'd forgotten to put the tickets in the box.

She heard the sound, too, as she brought in the bag of food, looked first at the door then at me and commented that the timing of our little naked escapade had been exceptionally good. Even I tried to smile.

The new arrival was a tall, thin, bearded bloke. A short exchange with him made it clear we didn't need to worry about the hut tickets. The guy introduced himself as Fabian from Austria, your typical hippie hiker. He said he'd come from Lake Angelus and had first thought he'd stop at John Tait Hut, three hours back down the road, but reckoned he'd still have enough daylight to get out this far. Pretty good estimate; outside the sky was already a dark shade of blue.

I poured water into the pot and left it to boil. I took out some rice cakes, the cheese and a packet of soup, then handed her the empty water bottle and instructed her to fill it up from the tank.

Fabian brought his hiking boots and poles inside, leaving them next to the door, and suggested we do the same. We'd thought it might be a good idea to air our boots, but then Fabian mentioned the keas.

As I lifted our boots and poles into the cabin, Fabian explained that once we were about a thousand metres up we were already in kea territory.

I told him I'd heard people talking about them back in Kepler.

Fabian said that in that case we probably knew what he was getting at.

The door opened, and she came back in with the bottle of water, batting sand flies out of the way and cursing like a trooper. In English she said that she couldn't understand why such an amazing country had to be full of creatures that were such arseholes. Fabian nodded, and they continued talking about the local fauna. I didn't really listen any more, but I was amused and slightly disappointed at her naïveté. Animals just follow the behavioural patterns typical of their species; they don't have morals. Only Disney films depict animals with a concept of good and evil.

Pizza boxes piled inside deep freezers. Packets of frozen chips stacked beside them.

My skin starts to tingle at once. Hollow, familiar. So sweet you want to scratch it.

I have a quick look around and kneel down. The cable winds its way behind the refrigerated drinks cabinet, supposedly out of sight. A sharp tug. Snap. It's out of the plug point.

An almost imperceptible hum in the soundscape of the store changes. Other than that, nothing happens. Somebody turns up. Lifts bags of frozen vegetables into their shopping trolley. They jangle icily. For now.

It'll take all day or even until the next morning for anyone to notice. The bags of fries will be mush. Toffee will ooze out of the ice-cream cones. Maybe a clock or an alarm will ring once the temperature inside starts to rise. But by then, with any luck, it'll be too late.

I pick up a large packet of crisps and a litre-and-a-half bottle of fizzy and take them to the check-out. The girl doesn't give me a second look. This isn't the shop where I've got an account.

Even if the stuff in the freezers don't thaw out entirely, there'll be no way of knowing how long the bags have been warm, whether they've gone off or not. Just imagine the fuss, the hoo-hah, the palaver. The staff will give each other the evil eye, then end up blaming the cleaners.

If the shopkeeper's a total tightarse he'll let the stuff freeze again and try to flog it off. Some shopper'll be in for a Kinder Surprise when they open their bag of chips, now nothing but furry ice crystals. Some kid'll end up with ice cream that's like candle wax.

I rip open the bag of crisps at the shop door; some of them spill on to the stairs. Let the pigeons have their share. I take a good handful of them and stuff them in my mouth so my teeth can hardly move.

Fizzy drinks taste best when the inside of your mouth is white with salt, your saliva glands clogged up.

SOUTH COAST TRACK, TASMINIA
Deadman's Bay
Wednesday, March 2007

HEIDI

The people here look like they're half dead. Grey in the face, and they don't talk much, can barely muster a passing, exhausted hi. One group at least asks whether it's a long way to the water source. I point back the way we came, towards the stream, and tell them it's about two hundred metres. Jyrki offers to show them the way; we need more water for tomorrow, too. There's another group of six just arriving, including a couple that are clearly well past middle age. They stumble with fatigue and don't bother looking for a suitable pitch, just shrug their rucksacks to the ground and sit down on or beside their bags to catch their breath, their faces buried in their hands, each of them plastered up to the armpits in mud and soaked through, although there hasn't been a drop of rain all day.

On top of their boots and trouser legs they're wearing gaiters, also coated in a thick layer of mud. We had a look at gaiters just like those at the Mountain Design store in Hobart, but Jyrki decided that they'd just be dead weight, only for people who wanted to play it safe.

All these people have crawled in here to spend the night after crossing the Ironbound Range from the opposite direction. Evening is already drawing in, and the camp's name is beginning to seem decidedly appropriate.

Jyrki is cooking dinner, mixing a packet of tuna into some instant mashed potato. Although he scrapes the packet clean with neurotic care, he still gives it a sceptical sniff.

'You always get flakes of fish stuck in the corners. In a few days they'll stink, and the possums will catch the scent immediately.'

He holds out the water bottle and tells me to take the bag a distance from the camp and wash it thoroughly.

I don't say a word; I just take it and go.

This is the second camp we've stayed in where you're theoretically allowed to start a campfire. Out of curiosity I take a look at the designated campfire spot to see whether it has been stocked with dry logs or whether one of the new arrivals has already started a fire. Then it wouldn't be our responsibility.

And anyway a plastic bag like that would burn in seconds; Jyrki would never have to know. There's an old pad of matches in my waist bag, left over from the occasional smoke on some past holiday. Jyrki keeps the lighter for himself.

The campfire spot is a large high ring of stones. Inside it are the charred remains from the last time it was used. The exhausted campers are busying themselves further off; I can see flashes of blue and orange through the foliage. However, I lose interest in our neighbours and the fire the minute I see something sticking out from between the stones in the ring.

Paper!

Real *bona fide* paper!

I don't know whether it's been left here for people to read or to be used as kindling. Perhaps it was meant to be read; at a cursory glance I can see that it talks about the finite number of places in paradise and about lions lying languidly beside the lambs. I'm not remotely interested in the text or its content, but in the softness of the yellowish, anything-but-shiny roughness of the pulp paper.

I stuff the paper into the pockets of my camp trousers, every last sheet. Five four-paged little pamphlets, made into A4s by folding them in half twice. Oh, I have a treasure; dearer it is than gold.

I'm in such a good mood that I relent and wash out the damn tuna packet. The bonfire is the best place for the few droplets of rinsing water I've used. No doubt the next fire there will destroy every last atom of tuna threatening to disrupt the fine balance of the local ecosystem.

We stopped, and the silence driven away by the stamping of our feet flowed back again from the recesses of the land.

— Joseph Conrad, *Heart of Darkness*

NEW ZEALAND
Nelson Lakes
February 2007

JYRKI

She was panting like a little horse, white spittle collecting around the edges of her mouth. But she didn't complain; just hauled herself up using her hands. Her hiking poles clanked against the rocks like chattering teeth as they dangled around her wrists.

Travers Saddle was the first mountain pass she'd crossed in her life.

And it was over seventeen hundred metres high. The terrain was similar to that in the Alps – every now and then we had to clamber up almost vertical rock faces – although in the Alps I'd never had to scale many slopes as challenging as these. This was no longer simply rambling; this was mountaineering.

You could just make out patches of snow at the top of the mountain.

We had a break once we got to the top; a muesli bar and some water. The views were impressive, but we could only rest for a few minutes. The eight-kilometre leg had taken us eight hours; that was reason enough not to sit about daydreaming.

The path down was nothing but a steep, loose scree. At times we were almost skating. Further down the slope the river had flooded big time. Without a decent map this path would have been all but invisible beneath all the trees that had been ripped up by their roots.

It was a hellish stretch.

And she didn't make a peep.

When day began to turn into afternoon, I suggested that maybe we shouldn't go to Angelus Lake but that we take the Circuit instead. The trail to Angelus was marked on the map as a particularly difficult route.

I imagined she wouldn't be that up for something even more challenging than this quite yet.

She didn't say anything, just gave a shake of the head and spluttered, and again she made me think of a horse – a small, stubborn pony. I wasn't sure whether the shake of the head was a yes or a no.

HEIDI

The trail to Sabine Hut wound its way through a valley, crossing some incredible bubbling gorge rivers on the way, the kinds of places that in Finland would instantly be turned into sites of national importance with local-history museums and inns serving traditional food. Crossing one of the gorges, we met a woman coming from the opposite direction. She chatted to us for a while, like everyone around here, and eventually asked us if we had any hut tickets.

What? Did she want to buy them from us? Then, to my embarrassment, I realized that she was a ranger – she had a DOC patch sewn on to the front of her Girl-Guide-brown shirt.

At West Sabine we had put four of our tickets into the box. Jyrki dug the remaining four out of his bag and showed them to the woman. In fluent English he explained that we were on our way to Speargrass Hut for the night and that from there it was only a short leap over to St Arnaud.

The woman nodded, indicated that Jyrki could put the tickets away and said something about us having a very long day ahead.

Jyrki waved his hand. I looked at him enquiringly, but his expression remained impassive. The woman bid us a good day.

Sabine Hut was located at perhaps the most beautiful spot imaginable, on the shores of Lake Rotoiti. The hut was big – it was more of a manor house – and boasted a large veranda and breathtaking views out across the lake. Reaching out into the open lake was a jetty inviting passing hikers to swim and row out into the water.

It would have been the most wonderful place in the world to spend the afternoon and the evening had it not been – like everywhere in New Zealand's southern island near water and not a thousand metres above sea level – the sand flies' very own Riviera.

We thought we'd seen sand flies at Upper Travers Hut, but this was something else entirely. The air was quite literally black. They were buzzing in heaving swarms. Bites like stinging electric shocks prickled all around us, tiny black spots pushing their way into our eyes, our mouths and our nostrils.

Once we had escaped into the hut, we saw that the situation indoors wasn't much better. Annoyingly, the door had been left open for the best part of the day. A stoical hiker sat on the upper bunk of one of the beds reading – perhaps he was a local who had developed some kind of immunity, or else he was a fakir looking for new and exciting ways to torture himself.

'We can't stay here,' I said, agonized, as we stuffed our mouths with rice cakes and dried fruit without enjoying them in the least. 'We just can't. We'll go crazy.'

'It's two o'clock. The sun won't set for another seven hours. We could reach Speargrass in that time.'

I couldn't help but give a smirk.

'Well, that's what you told the ranger.'

If Jyrki was capable of blushing, he blushed right then.

'Are you up for it?'

Well, what do you know? The first time he'd ever asked me that question.

'We've got to. There can't be anything worse than this.'

How little I knew.

Needless to say, the trail immediately turned into a gallant incline that continued for hours and hours. On top of that it was extremely ragged and difficult to traverse — clearly it had been trodden much less than the trails we had seen during the previous days. The strangest thing was that the whole forest seemed hollow; our hiking poles sunk deep into the ground in the oddest places, and between the roots of trees we could see hollows, some the size of caves. Jyrki explained that this could have been the site of an enormous landslide and that the forest could have grown on top of the displaced soil.

Our progress was eerily slow and difficult, staggering and stumbling all the way, and we didn't speak for hours, the only sounds being our gasping and cursing and the occasional clank of pole against rock.

And all the while the trail continued inexorably upwards — even, unforgiving, draining.

The rest of the world was nowhere, as far as our eyes and ears were concerned. Just nowhere. Gone, disappeared; swept off without leaving a whisper or a shadow behind, Joseph whispered in my ears.

The trek up to Travers Saddle had been a brisk, relatively demanding stroll; this, on the other hand, was nothing short of a slow, torturous death.

My hands were so sticky with sweat that my fingers stuck to one another. My shins were two lifeless logs, moving one after the other only because they could no longer stop.

By the time we arrived in Speargrass there was barely an hour of daylight left.

There they are, rows of silent, self-satisfied lumps. Black, red, dark green. Darker colours are the best. With lighter ones you can't really see nothing.

You can use a stone or a Swiss Army knife, but an ordinary large nail is the best of all. You can find them on the ground, usually next to some old demolished house. Rusty and bent. They fit nicely at the bottom of your pocket.

First clench the nail in your fist so that either the tip or the head is jutting out between your fingers. Then walk past the car slowly. If you're lucky and act cool, even if someone sees you, no one will even clock what you're doing. There's a soft sound as the paintwork peels off. Sometimes the sound is more shrill and metallic; sometimes you can barely hear a thing. Sometimes the nail slips around infuriatingly and you have to press harder. At night, or if the car is parked out of sight, you can try to take off the mirrors or at least spruce 'em up a bit for good measure.

It's not about envy. When people see a clean single-coloured wall somewhere in town it's not out of envy at the wall's pristine condition that they pick up a can of spray paint and draw a tag or a picture of a pussy. They just want to leave their mark on the world.

SOUTH COAST TRACK, TASMANIA
Deadman's Bay
Thursday, March 2007

JYRKI

The next morning she seems pretty motivated, although it's early and she should understand well enough by now that Ironbound is nasty.

You can't set up camp halfway across it. There's no even ground, and once you get up on the ridge there's no water either. Out here the fixed campsites aren't just more of the same over-the-top mollycoddling; they are, quite simply, the only places where there's a reliable brook and enough flat ground to put up a tent.

She wants coffee instead of tea. I prefer tea. Still, we have to come to some kind of compromise, as teabags and sachets of instant coffee all have to be shared.

The smell of coffee is all-pervading; it doesn't belong in the breaking dawn. It makes me think of the city; latte-faces sitting around outside Starbucks.

I'd set the mobile to wake us up at half past five, to give us plenty of time. Without a GPS, the alarm-clock function is the only use for a mobile phone out here. It feels odd being in a place where the air isn't thick with signals. How do we know what kind of invisible nerve poisons they're cunningly feeding us — odourless, tasteless but as corrosive as radioactive fall-out? Wireless technology has been developed little by little, so much so that soon it'll meet the fate of the *Megaloceros giganteus*: in order to secure its survival, evolution required that the animal grow larger and larger sets of antlers until finally the entire Irish elk species collapsed under the weight of its own puffed-up majesty.

Crossing Ironbound can take up to ten hours. She says she needs the toilet. I ask her why she doesn't just go in the bushes. She mumbles something about a number two.

I'm ready to leave. Waiting around eats away at my time and motivation.

The pit toilet is at the end of a path marked with a couple of plastic orange ribbons. She wanders off, checking her pockets on the way: making sure she's got her paper tissues. Mine are already gone. I'll have to remember to stock up from hers.

Now I understand why she wanted coffee. My stomach is telling me that coffee gets things moving in your gut.

HEIDI

The pamphlets rustle in my pockets as I crouch down in the grass and throw up the morsel of flatbread and the cheese I've had for breakfast. Even as it rises up my throat, the vomit still smells of granulated coffee. The food hasn't had time to be digested, so I kick at the dried leaves to hide the spatter of sick.

I've completely forgotten about going to the loo; or rather, I haven't forgotten about it, but it'll have to bloody wait.

The lid of the pit toilet, knocked together from some rotten planks of wood, is still open behind me; I can feel the smell in my nose and try to breathe through my mouth to stave off another gag reflex. I wipe the string of saliva dangling from the side of my mouth with a rough piece of pamphlet. I slowly stagger to my feet, trying not to look down into the pit as I throw in the piece of paper and slide the lid back on with my foot.

But I can't help seeing down there, there in the brightening light of the Tasmanian morning.

Only a hand's width away from the edge of the pit is a heaving mass of pure brown liquid shit. And the mass is swarming and buzzing, literally boiling, so that its surface is teeming and twirling with large fat white maggots.

I shunt the lid into place, turn and crouch down again, but there's nothing in my stomach but yellow bile.

By the time I get back to the camp, there's a bitter acidic taste in my mouth. Jyrki jumps to his feet from the tree trunk he's been sitting on and glances at his watch.

I can't tell him. I think of Conrad.

'Men who come out here should have no entrails.' He sealed the utterance with that smile of his, as though it had been a door opening into a darkness he had in his keeping.

'I've got to wash my hands. Will you pour?'

Jyrki nods with a sigh – more time-wasting. I can feel beads of sweat appear on my forehead when I go to look for the wombat bottle in the side pocket of my rucksack, but it's not there.

'Where's the wombat bottle?'

Jyrki shrugs his shoulders. 'I haven't used it.'

'You fetched the water last night.'

'It was a deep brook. You could hold bottles under the water. I used the bigger bottles and the Platypus.'

'So where is it then?'

I search everywhere; I look under the bushes and behind the trees. I remember that the bottle was empty when we arrived at the camp; I'd taken it out of my shorts pocket when I got changed. Where had I put it? Next to the bigger bottles in the vestibule, like I always did? I can't remember for sure; it's become such a routine.

'Follow your tracks. But, hey, we haven't got time for this. I'm more concerned that you've dropped it in the first place. As far as the environment is concerned, human beings are nothing but sum of their excretions, and now that bottle is just a piece of non-biodegradable rubbish in completely the wrong place – and it was left there by you.'

I can feel my eyes itching and stinging, my lower eyelids filling. I feel bad as it is. Jyrki is pouring water on to my hands from the Platypus. I rub them together long and hard, almost devoutly, as if I were cleansing myself of what I'd seen a moment ago, and wipe my hands on my shorts. I pick up the Platypus and take a couple of long gulps of water, although I can see from Jyrki's expression that he thinks we should have saved those few drops for when we're on the road. I hand the bottle back to him and have a last look behind our tree-trunk seats.

'I've had that bottle from the minute we arrived in Australia.'

'A freebie given out on the plane. It would be another thing if we'd lost a lighter or an army knife. Besides, you should never become too attached to inanimate objects.'

. . . *everything belonged to him. It made me hold my breath in expectation of hearing the wilderness burst into a prodigious peal of laughter that would shake the fixed stars in their places. Everything belonged to him — but that was a trifle. The thing was to know what he belonged to, how many powers of darkness claimed him for their own.*

— Joseph Conrad, *Heart of Darkness*

NEW ZEALAND
Nelson Lakes, Speargrass Hut
February 2007

JYRKI

The hut at Speargrass was crammed to the rafters. After the roominess at West Sabine, and especially at Upper Travers Hut, walking into this place was like being slapped across the face with a wet towel. When I saw how crowded it was I considered putting up the tent, but there wouldn't have been a decent pitch. The area around the hut was bobbled with clumps of grass, rough hillocks the size of your head every metre or so.

It turned out that most of the people in the hut were there for a party – a hen party, of all things.

You must be a real Kiwi if your idea of fun is dragging sacks full of dishes and pans, tinned food and fresh vegetables a good three hours from the nearest village. Or, more to the point, an hour and a half from the nearest car park. Then there are the sleeping-bags and all manner of other paraphernalia. Then you have fun all by yourselves in a hut where there's barely room to move.

There were about a dozen women in the hen-party crowd. All the others in the hut were either lone hikers or couples. As we arrived the evening sky was already turning a dark shade of blue, so we were by default the last ones in.

There wasn't any room for our rucksacks by the wall. We tried to rest them against other people's stuff so that they wouldn't be in the way. They had to be taken out for the night anyway, but it's just nicer to do some things in the warm.

Then I saw the bunks. Every mattress had a bag, a pillow or a sleeping-bag on it. I tried to count how many people there were in the hut and how many berths there were; the numbers didn't match, but perhaps there were still some people outside. I told her this, and she nodded. The disappointment in her eyes was bottomless.

HEIDI

Everyone was fussing around the kitchen worktops or sitting eating or reading at the table in the long cabin. We stood in the middle of the room for a good while before anyone even looked at us. Nobody budged from the bench. Nobody moved closer to the person sitting next to them, not even to create the illusion that they were trying to make space for us. If I picked up on any kind of signal at our arrival, it was the message of barely hidden contempt shining from their faces: What the hell are they doing coming in here at this time?

Jyrki started rummaging in his rucksack, took out his mug and the bag with his change of clothes and stepped outside without saying a word. I stood where I was and sensed the sweat turning cold on my clothes, and with it a sense of paralysis flowed into my limbs. I was stiff, right through to my bones, numb and aching. Jyrki came back almost immediately, his brow furrowed.

'The water tank was empty.'

'How's that possible?'

'There are probably more people at this place than at the other huts.' He shrugged his shoulders. 'Or else someone's left the tap dripping or washed their dishes using too much running water. But there's a brook down there.' He looked around and sniffed. 'Well, I'll bet you if I started running about here in the buff I'd be out of here before you could say sexual-harassment charges.'

I gave a start, and mixed with the feeling of chill and irritation and hunger and muscle ache came the memory of what this trip had cost me, and I couldn't bring myself to laugh at Jyrki's joke, although I appreciated he was only trying to lighten the mood.

There was nothing I wanted less than to walk down to the brook, but we needed water, and anything would have been preferable to the stiff atmosphere in the hut – so thick with rejection that when we opened the door it felt like poking our heads out of a viscous jelly.

The brook was wide, clear and lively, although it was pretty far away from the cabin. From the bank you almost couldn't make out the cabin at all against the darkening sky. Nearer to the cabin was a small ditch, muddy, narrow and overgrown. Somebody from the cabin was standing there filling her cooking pot with water.

'Idiots,' Jyrki scoffed.

Taking off my sticky clothes felt awful, and the first mugful of cold water on my face and neck even worse, but after a moment it felt as though the water had flowed through my skin and was now roaring in my veins, as searing as pure alcohol, and when I stood up to dry myself my cheeks were red, my heart was pounding; the icy wind felt cooling and refreshing against my skin, and I was ready to go back into the hut, be there dragons or not.

We cooked our noodles and ate our rice cakes – standing up, of course, until a couple of our fellow cabin residents returned to their mattresses to read by the light of their headlamps, and we could finally rest our backsides on the edge of one of the kitchen benches. We washed our dishes and brushed our teeth outside, and when we came back into the cabin I realized that everybody was inside by now. People had already retired to their bunks, some had slid inside their sleeping-bags, and the only people still giggling and chatting inanely were the hen-night crowd. Candles were lit on the table, and the bride-to-be – for whom, up here at an altitude of over a thousand metres, someone had been bothered to lug a plastic tiara – was subjected to a number of long, complicated tests, tarot readings, you name it, all of which invariably resulted in volleys of feigned virginal sniggers.

One of the mattresses must have been free. Simply counting the number of people in the cabin was enough to work it out, but it had been very cleverly covered with bundles of clothes and all manner of other stuff. Although I tried to stare meaningfully at the berth, when I finally went and sat on it out of sheer bloody-mindedness nobody offered to move any of the junk away.

I wasn't planning on asking whether the place was taken or not. I could only imagine the general sense of irritation, the scowling that would have made the air in the cabin even stickier and turned us into even larger and more shapeless lumps of solidified intrusion than we already were.

In any case, there was only one free mattress – although all the mattresses were laid next to one another, forming a single soft surface. It wouldn't have caused a great deal of discomfort to them if everyone had shifted ten centimetres towards their neighbour to make some more room. Both of us would have fitted into the newly created space.

There were very clear rules in these cabins: first come, first served, no reservations, not even for a friend turning up later on. And, when the cabin is overcrowded, you're supposed to make room.

Apparently they hadn't bothered reading the latter rule on the list, although the first rule was clearly to be strictly upheld.

For a moment I wondered whether or not to check for hut tickets. I was sure there would be people who hadn't paid – I couldn't see any ticket stubs dangling from their straps or rucksack buckles. After checking the bags, I'd inform them all that in these situations it's clear that paying customers take preference.

Who did I think I was kidding? If I couldn't bring myself to point out the fact of the unfairly reserved berth, how could I suddenly turn into a self-appointed ranger? And the wave of anger and disapproval that would undoubtedly follow would be enough to make you choke.

We stared at the floor.

In a way, it seemed symptomatic of these people's indifference that no one had noticed we were speaking Finnish. Normally this was a sure-fire conversation-opener. Hey, what kind of language is that? We spoke in muttered, hushed voices, as though we were suddenly ashamed of our own language, too. Perhaps we were.

'There's nothing else for it.'

'No.'

We dug out our sleeping-mats – all the while overly aware of the noise we were causing, our movements filling the air space, and trying to minimize the fuss as much as possible – and inflated them. We couldn't go next to the benches because there was a constant flow of people going to and fro into the kitchen area. For the same reason we couldn't go next to the door. Not next to the bunks, that was for sure, as anyone might have to leave their bed and get up in the middle of the night.

The only place we could find was half covered by the kitchen worktops. As we were laying out our mats and sleeping-bags I could feel that we were being watched all the time, and whenever I tried to return the gaze I noticed that eyes were turned away suddenly and deliberately to one side. We're not getting your hints, their eyes were telling me.

I crawled inside my sleeping-bag. Already I could feel the draught coming up through the floorboards. Beneath my thin mat the planks felt very, very hard.

Jyrki gave me a kiss, then zipped himself inside his own sleeping-bag like an Egyptian mummy.

At first I tried to read Conrad, but it was too dark, and taking out my headlamp would have attracted as much hostile attention as a lighthouse. I tried to close my eyes, but the shrieks and sniggers from the hen-party table only seemed to increase, at times even bursting into song. Their enjoyment seemed to be blown out of all proportion, considering that, at least as far as I could see, they hadn't brought a drop of alcohol with them to Speargrass Hut.

Then the traffic started.

All of a sudden, almost all of the women in the hen-party group had things to do in the kitchen area. Fetching one thing, bringing another, looking for matches, candles, bags of crisps. Their feet hit us in the ribs, back, almost in the head; the girls were very uninhibited and utterly unapologetic. What have you gone and laid down there for, the feet were saying loud and clear.

It was well into the early hours of the morning by the time the last of the bridesmaids had stopped whispering and giggling in their bunks.

Everything was silent, and I needed the toilet.

Outside the moon was shining.

It was pretty damned beautiful.

I couldn't be bothered to climb the steps up to the outhouse but crouched down next to the porch. As I clambered back towards the door, I suddenly remembered.

At first it came to me because of the mountains, then because of Conrad.

The earth seemed unearthly. We are accustomed to look upon the shackled form of a conquered monster, but there — there you could look at a thing monstrous and free.

I remembered what Fabian had told me.

The keas.

The keas, those mean, intelligent birds.

The hen party's things were on the veranda, to the left of the door. I knew this because the girls had been going in and out all night to collect various things, to go to the toilet, and on their way tying their shoes or rummaging in their bags right over there.

Now I had a beak.

Now I had claws.

I ruffled my feathers in the night air and the pale golden moonlight shining across the glens. My wings fluttered for a moment before closing shut in a quiver.

I reached out a long agile limb.

A shoe lace, just like that.

A backpack buckle open, just like that, and what item would it be particularly annoying to lose? Keys? Absolutely. Car keys? Now that would be a shame.

The insole of a shoe left out to air, just like that; looks like it was one of those special-shaped ones, maybe even made to measure. Shit happens.

A few more shoe laces, clothes yanked out of an open bag, spilt out like colourful bowels – who knows where the wind might carry them? The capricious New Zealand wind.

Our boots were inside, and the rucksacks we'd left on the veranda were securely covered. Of course, I pulled back the covers over our bags, too, picked at them with my quick, nimble and oh-so-nifty claws and opened up a few zips: our things had to be touched as well, that was clear. But we didn't lose anything; our luck was in.

I went back into the cabin, which was now filled with the sound of sniffling, gentle snoring and the smell of farts and candle wax, and once I had crawled back into my sleeping-bag I fell asleep like a contented child.

'Kea: The Open-Programme Bird'
by Jiselle Ruby and Anthony Verloc

The kea belongs to a group of animal species that can well be compared to humans, inasmuch as its ability to adapt to changing conditions, such as the diminishing of their living environment or the arrival of new sources of nutrition, is both fast and exceptionally efficient. The kea's resilience as a species is based on its resourcefulness and opportunism, qualities which some researchers now believe can no longer be considered simply instinctual actions.

The kea is the only species of mountain parrot in the world. It lives primarily in the uplands of the South Island of New Zealand, often above the snowline, and generally in such harsh natural conditions that the acquisition of sustenance represents a significant challenge in itself. For this reason, the kea has developed into a master of survival.

The kea's diet is normally plant based, consisting of various seeds, nuts, shoots, etc., although it should be noted that it is exceptionally flexible with regard to its diet and is eager to seek out alternative sources of nourishment. In fact, the kea will eat almost anything that comes its way and switches readily to animal proteins whenever they are available.

The kea is a very lively creature and always seems in need of challenging activity. If food is readily available, it spends a greater proportion of its time engaged in other activities such as social games and competitions. It would appear that these games and displays of prowess in part serve to create and maintain hierarchical relationships within the flock.

The kea is an extremely inquisitive bird – a trait that is clearly a key factor in the survival of the species – and can even solve complicated problems with relative ease. When it encounters an unfamiliar object, the kea will normally examine it carefully, often by breaking it into pieces. This behavioural pattern becomes more common when food is in greater supply, meaning that the bird's energy is not spent searching for its daily nourishment.

SOUTH COAST TRACK, TASMANIA
Deadman's Bay to Louisa River
Thursday, March 2007

JYRKI

I look up and squint. How the hell could anyone ever think of going through that?

Then, after a moment, the eye latches on a tree root that might serve as a wobbly step, or makes out a hole in the rocks big enough for the tip of a boot, and with considerable effort, all but crawling, we manage to inch our way forward. There's water running down the path. Further up on the ridge it must be raining.

The path is a stream is a path. In this terrain it's the only track there is.

The path is a sick joke.

When you look up you can't see the sky, because the steep, almost vertical wall that is Ironbound, with its giant intertwining sodden trees and bushes, both in front of us and above us, *are* the sky. The ridge almost seems to fall in on top of us with its crushing gloominess. Even at midday there's so little light in this all but sheer tree tunnel that everything is shrouded in a greenish darkness.

And even when we're not hauling ourselves up across this hybrid of way and waterway the shelf-like plateaux in between them are nothing but immense quagmires. The mud is black, churned into a thick porridge. And it's bloody deep. You can't avoid it or walk around it. The only thing you can do is look for roots or branches sticking out beneath the enormous pools of slurry, trampled clumps of grass or, if you're lucky, a blessed stone to stop your feet sinking too far into the depths.

The myriad tree roots stretching out into the path are like very cleverly designed hurdles or traps. They offer your boots about as much friction as a bar of soap. They are elevated either just enough so that you trip over them or just enough that you have to make an effort to step over them. They form tangled networks, the gaps in between them just too small to put your boot through but large enough that they could twist your ankle into the most contorted positions.

On top of that, this joke of a path is pinned down with a fair number of impressive-sized fallen trees forming sheer walls or barriers as thick as your waist. There's no option but to climb over them and force your way through the thick branches for all you're worth.

HEIDI

Jyrki uses his hiking pole to support him on the other side of a fallen tree. He apparently feels something firm beneath the surface and lowers almost his entire body-weight on to his pole. There comes a yell as he disappears behind the tree trunk, followed by a sticky squelch as he hits the ground on his side. His pole is stuck into the ground almost up to the handle. Jyrki hauls himself upright and, cursing and standing up to his groin in mud, tries to wrench his pole up from the sludge. But the mire just burps and gurgles, as if some creature living inside the earth didn't want let go of the strange titanium-aluminium object that had suddenly been thrust into its underground kingdom.

Jyrki yanks at his pole, cursing profusely. If I weren't so weak with a sore stomach and standing up to my ankles in mud myself, I might even have suppressed a laugh. Seeing as we've stopped, I take the opportunity to crouch down for a piss in the middle of the path. I don't bother taking off the rucksack, although the struggle to stand upright once more makes my thigh muscles recoil. Taking the thing off and heaving it back on to my shoulders would require way too much effort.

The first leg of our hike across Queen Charlotte Track in New Zealand had been a bit muddy towards the end, but compared with this it was a breeze. Here, if you put your foot down in the wrong spot you could be up to your thighs in squelching sludge.

It'll soon be time to suggest stopping for a bite to eat; there hasn't been anything in my stomach all morning, save for those couple of minutes. We've been moving uphill for three hours, but it seems we're not even halfway up the steeper-than-thou incline at Ironbound. The forest is damp and thick and ugly, rising like a wall on both sides; mud churning all around us and nowhere to put our rucksacks down. If we want to eat or do anything more complicated than thrashing about in the undergrowth, we'll have to balance our rucksacks against a tree trunk and do whatever it is we have to do standing up, shifting from one foot to the other.

I'm beyond caring. I just keep moving through the bush and mud without thinking about the amount of shit my boots are gobbling up, stumbling and bruising myself, swallowing back the tears and four-letter words — anything, so long as Jyrki behind me doesn't notice how I'm panting, my mouth wide open, almost hyperventilating, whimpering like a woman in labour.

When it gets even worse I start thinking about Dad — his arrogant face, his fat fingers bulging beneath his signet rings, his hands, quick to punish and quick to buy the kind of behaviour he wanted — and the thought makes me lift my feet again and again and push forwards instead of slumping into a weeping wreck in the mire at the edge of the path.

My shorts are caked in all manner of dirt and slime from the slippery tree trunks, and I curse myself for not putting on a pair of trekking trousers. At least they would have protected me a bit instead of letting all the branches and thorns tear at me, scratching my shins with uninhibited abandon.

Gaiters dead weight? Yeah, right.

Well well, Jyrki happens to like the suggestion of a break, too — a change of clothes and a few apricots, although apparently we have to save our muesli bars for the top of ridge once we reach the majestic altitude of nine hundred metres. I pull on my trekking trousers at the edge of the path, at times balancing on one leg. I have to take my boots off because they won't fit through the trouser legs. Besides, even if the trousers had had some ingenious zip system to help you push your boots down the legs without taking them off, you'd be mad to shove clumps of wet humus through the insides of your trousers. Meanwhile Jyrki takes a look at his hiking pole.

'Fucking, fucking *fuck*.'

Well, that certainly comes right from the heart. I turn to look at him. The tip of his telescopic trekking pole is missing.

'Fucking cock-sucking arsewipe. I wondered why the terrain seemed so fucking wonky on one side.'

The mud has swallowed up the entire lower section of the pole; the sludge has won the tug-of-war, at the same time scoring a resounding victory over the Komperdell spring mechanism.

I've never heard Jyrki swear so much. He unscrews the remaining telescope section of the pole as far out as it will go, so that it will be of at least some use alongside its intact partner. The severed pole looks weirdly crippled, and because the broken end is open like a pipe you can expect it to take a neat mud sample every time it sinks into the ground.

'Fucking useless piece of shit.'

'You shouldn't get too attached to inanimate objects,' I comment, poker-faced, with a knowing nod of the head.

JYRKI

Once we move above the treeline we find ourselves in the clouds, completely enveloped in mist. Visibility is only a couple of metres. Once the forest disappears it is swiftly replaced with boggy marshlands. There must be some directive to protect sensitive alpine plants and vegetation, as the path continues in steps along a series of duckboards, all the while moving in a steep incline.

It's almost a relief. At least on these steps you can sit down for a moment, take a good gulp of water and unwrap a muesli bar.

The air has been damp throughout this leg. Now the water is starting to condense into droplets on my arms and in my hair. It's only once you stop for a minute that you realize how cold it is. Out here, climbing up to eight hundred metres has the same effect as climbing two thousand in the Alps. I have to put my jacket on straight away.

When there are no trees there's nothing to hold back the wind. It comes right in across the sea. This high up you get a real sense of its ferocity, biting and penetrating. The strongest gusts can make you stagger to maintain your balance.

The wind isn't just wind. It's cutting. It howls and gnaws.

Never was suncream as pointless as today.

I try to chew the muesli bar, but my mouth is almost too dry. I wonder what's wrong with my eyes. Why does the surrounding mist suddenly seem so stripy? Then it dawns on me: it's raining harder now, and the water is coming down as sleet. Horizontally. Or snow. Or hail. In its solid form, the water strikes my cheek facing towards the sea with such force that a moment later the flesh is tingling and sore.

I look at my hiking poles, particularly the crippled one, and it pisses me off so much it hurts.

I pull up the hood on my hiking jacket and stuff the muesli-bar wrapper into my pocket. I grab my poles and stand up.

'The path won't walk itself,' I tell her.

HEIDI

As I sit down on a duckboard step I see that the stitching in the seam of one of my trouser legs has come apart. It's gaping open almost right up to the knee.

'Tasmania ruins everything.'

'What?' Jyrki is already on his feet, gazing up ahead of us as if he could actually see anything in this weather.

It's an irony of almost cosmic proportions that Ironbound, supposedly the breathtaking highpoint in the panoramas along the whole of South Coast Track, is completely shrouded by the cloud cover, with whirling snow hurtling into our faces more convincingly than Finnish storms in March ever do nowadays on the other side of the planet.

It occurs to me that, in addition to the mud, the water and snow now have free access to the mouth of one of my boots.

And when I stand up I realize that it's all in there already and has been for a while, that the heat of my body movement has prevented me from noticing that my boot is full of water.

Jyrki looks at my trouser leg and shows me one of his hiking poles. There's something silvery grey wrapped around the middle.

'There's a couple of metres of duct tape on here. You can fix it with that.'

But the idea of taking my trousers off in this blizzard seems impossible, and I say so.

Jyrki shrugs his shoulders. My unstitched trouser leg billows like a sail with every step I take.

JYRKI

You could almost imagine a small dinosaur peering out from behind a rock at any moment.

Ironbound's western face is virtually the Garden of Eden. The path winds its way along the edge of a ravine so deep that you can't see the bottom through the mist. Just over a metre wide, this shelf of rock is home to a gushing profusion of all different shades of green, buds and shoots in red, lilac, yellow, the orange of pine needles. The dampness and the mist in the background make the colours seem even deeper and more exuberant. Battered by the wind, the flora here is close to the ground, but it is incredibly diverse and comes in forms I've never seen before. Perhaps this is what the world looked like some time back in the Mesozoic era. In its sheer colourfulness and strangeness, this is another Tasmania altogether; it couldn't be more different from the almost savannah-like yellowy-green landscapes of the plains, the eucalyptus groves, the bushes and the scrub. Up here enormous boulders balance precariously on the edge of the cliff; sheer drops and promontories follow one after the other. Everywhere you look you can see that 18,000 years ago the land was covered with a continental ice sheet.

A primordial forest hanging on the edge of bottomless gorges, set right in the middle of a giants' game of skittles. Now I understand why Southy is cut the way it is.

As we descend further down the western face and the path begins to veer to the north-east, the flora thins out in stages. Soon the wall is almost nothing but rock. There is nothing to remind us of the suffocating black, damp forest of the eastern face. Now there are only long-suffering clumps of grass and every now and then a small stunted bush, ravaged by the wind, barely the height of a dwarf birch.

The sleet begins to relent, and the covering of clouds breaks in places. The glow of the sun can be seen as a pale moon-like disk behind the layer of clouds. After a moment I catch a glimpse of the sea looming to our left.

Christ alive.

We've crossed Ironbound.

HEIDI

It would have been a damned sight easier to come up this ridge than to go down it, and now I understand why there are so many people coming from the opposite direction and so few going the same way as us.

Who would have thought I'd end up actually missing the tree roots we had seen on the way up, the branches and the stone steps as high as your waist? This fresh nightmare, which we might jokingly call the descent path, is nothing more than a strip of gravel, worn away and slightly lighter than the rest of the cliff, running down the steep hillside that we're supposed to use to get back down without loose stones slipping beneath the soles of our feet or the weight of our rucksacks throwing us on to our backs. Our trekking poles are pretty useless, too – the only way to move forwards is to take small steps with the sides of your boots, like a first-time skier on an almost vertical expanse of snow.

My boot goes *slosh*. I can feel the muddy water churning inside my sock and between my toes. The other boot is probably full of all kinds of things, too, but at least it's drier.

The path of the Louisa River can be seen down below – not the actual river itself, of course, but the mass of thick vegetation that follows all the waterways around here. And I can see the start of tomorrow's leg: the undulating, yellowy-green plains which extend as far as the eye can see. Once we reach flatter ground it looks like it's only a stone's throw to the camp at Louisa River.

Thank God.

I suppose this must make me an 'experienced hiker'. That's the yardstick Jyrki had used before we came out here.

Is that how it happens, in just a few days? Is walking a certain number of kilometres sufficient to make you experienced, although there will be some sorts of terrain you've never hiked through? If you've spent ten years trekking through the backwoods of Lapland, does that make you an 'experienced hiker' in the Dolomites? Or vice versa? Or does 'experience' mean that you've learnt to appreciate certain theoretical rules of play (Jyrki's rules, that is, from which, in his vast experience, he often strays because a sufficient understanding of the rules naturally gives you the freedom to break them) from which you wouldn't dream of deviating: never leave the marked route or try to take a shortcut; be realistic about how much ground you can cover in a day's leg, and leave yourself plenty of time; drink lots of fluids; eat enough; learn to read a map and use a compass; learn the basics of first aid; learn to read the weather.

Is experience the fact that I've now picked up the masculine habit of hacking up the saliva in my mouth and spitting it at the side of the path, a habit that has become so routine I'm afraid I won't even notice I'm doing it once I'm back in the city?

I'm beginning to understand. My experience is in my toughened calf muscles and my breathing, which flows better with every day's walking. Without Kepler and Nelson Lakes – as piss-easy as Jyrki claimed they were – I would never have been able to cross Ironbound.

No matter how much I'd thought of Daddy Dearest.

Had I, in some unfathomable way, been given back my freedom after all?

We were wanderers on a prehistoric earth, on an earth that wore the aspect of an unknown planet. We could have fancied ourselves the first of men taking possession of an accursed inheritance, to be subdued at the cost of profound anguish and of excessive toil.

— Joseph Conrad, *Heart of Darkness*

AUSTRALIA
Grampians National Park, Hall's Gap
March 2007

JYRKI

We were sitting with Bill on the terrace of Tim's Place drinking God-awful canned Fosters. We'd got off the bus from Adelaide and jumped on Bill's minibus. Bill's company ran nature and sightseeing trips lasting a few days at a time, and they were also a handy way of getting from place to place. The next day his minibus would take us to the western end of the Great Ocean Walk. That was to be our first leg since arriving in Australia. Further inland it was still far too hot and dry to think about going on any of the bush walks. Along the coast it would be cooler, and we would be more certain of a regular water supply.

All the guidebooks had sung the praises of the Great Ocean Walk. It was one of the newer and most breathtaking of the average-length treks in mainland Australia, over ninety kilometres of national park coastal panoramas. The route featured climbs, dunes, caves and a few small villages that were worth seeing in their own right.

Here in the pass at Hall's Gap the night was pitch black.

By the time we had arrived in the forests of the Grampians it was already dark. Bill told us to look out of the windows for wallabies illuminated in the bus's headlights. He gave his passengers instructions. If you see a wallaby on the left, you shout out '*Left!*' If you see one on the right, shout '*Right!*' 'What if we see one straight ahead?' someone asked. Apparently then you shout '*Oh shit!*'

We'd bought food and drink on the way. Bill had told us that none of the restaurants in Hall's Gap would be open by the time we arrived. In any case, he said, there were far fewer than there used to be. It didn't matter: the backpackers' hostel had the usual shared kitchen.

The other minibus passengers had already hit the sack, but we had stayed up sipping our lagers. Bill had sat down to join us. A thick candle flickering in the breeze lit our table.

Bill was in his fifties, and he clearly had the gift of the gab. He was just telling us about how he had dealt with a couple who had started getting down to business on the back seat of his minibus (accelerating then braking until the couple fell off the seat and took the hint) when the night was pierced with a high-pitched, electronic noise.

Bill groaned and fished in the pocket of his khakis for his mobile phone, the screen of which gave off a ghostly phosphorescent glow. I was surprised when he handed it to me. He asked me to read the text message he had just received – he had left his glasses inside somewhere. I took the phone and told him the message was from someone called Lisa. Bill nodded. I pressed the button to bring up the text. I looked at it, then at Bill, then back at the message. My voice went hoarse as I read it out.

Bill pressed his hands against his eyes, just for a moment, then took them away, caught his breath, and all of a sudden the wrinkles beneath his eyes and around the edges of his mouth seemed deeper than before.

In 2006, a year ago, starting on 20 January, the Grampians had caught fire and burnt for two weeks solid. The diameter of the affected area was 360 kilometres.

It was hard to comprehend, until you realized that back home it would have meant the whole of southern Finland being ablaze right the way up to Jyväskylä and beyond.

Hundreds of thousands of hectares of forest had been destroyed, but, as if by a miracle, only two people had died, a father and son who had been trapped in their car by the flames. Around 60,000 sheep had perished. Nobody had bothered counting the wallabies.

It was no wonder that the flourishing tourist trade in Hall's Gap had started to fall apart.

And now Otway was on fire.

Otway was on fire, villages had already been evacuated, and Bill had no choice but to choose an alternative route.

The Great Ocean Walk would be closed off to us.

We were supposed to see koalas there, wild koalas living in trees.

I clenched my fists.

Although I'd known all of this beforehand.

How the soil was impoverished, how the hooves and trotters that this land should never have known trampled the soil, making it lifeless and barren. How the small furry animals tilling the land in search of food ended up in the mouths of rats and foxes artificially introduced into the country's ecosystem. How the ancient forests were decimated to such an extent that there were no great fire-resistant trees left, leaving fragile new growth all the more vulnerable to every spark.

That's how Australia will blaze.

That's how the world will be burnt.

She asked me what we should do now. I told her we were in the wrong part of the continent to bother with Bibbulmun Track. Of its impressive 900-kilometre stretch, there were a couple of hundred kilometres that ran along the coastline, which meant, theoretically, it would have been suitable for us given the time of year. But because Bibbulmun was a long way from the south-western corner of Australia for the time being we were through with mainland Australia.

It was just a question of distance. We could take Bill's minibus as far as Melbourne, jump on the Spirit of Tasmania ferry and chug all the way to Devonport.

It was time to go, a little ahead of schedule, to Tasmania and the Overland Track.

HEIDI

The landscape was incredible, a surreal mixture of black and green, so bright that it hurt the eyes.

Fresh shoots seemed to burst forth from the blackened, truncated stumps of the eucalyptus trees. The clumps of grass stood out so vividly against the pitch-black ground that they looked as though they had been lit up from the inside.

'There are some species sprouting here that have never been seen before round these parts. Some seeds apparently need the heat of a fire before they're able to germinate.'

Bill had driven through the Grampians a few days after they had finally managed to put the fire out.

'Imagine,' he said, his voice low, and I didn't know whether it was with anger or admiration, 'imagine this landscape, reaching out as far as the eye can see, and not a colour in sight. Nothing. It was as if you'd just taken a car and driven into a black-and-white film. All around you, nothing but black and grey. Residual smoke even blocked out the colour of the sky.' Bill coughed. 'Some of the eucalyptus trees were so old they didn't catch fire at first, but they have a habit of going hollow in the middle. The living part of the tree is just a thin layer beneath the bark. It was only a matter of time before the fire was sucked into their rotten insides and shot upwards. The upper branches were destroyed, but the trunks survived. The trees were like factory chimneys, black and sturdy, and you could see gloomy dark-grey smoke billowing out of their tops long after the fire itself had been put out. And there were thousands of those chimneys, thousands of them, stretching from here right to the horizon.'

Silence descended for a moment, as now we could envisage it and understand why this forest was so low and stunted.

'What was the name of that bloke? The European guy that used to draw pictures of hell?'

'Gustave Doré?' I suggested.

'Doré. That must be who I was thinking of. We should have invited the guy to take a look around. His drawings are pretty lame compared to what it was like out here.'

'The Land of Mordor?' some Tolkien fan shouted from further back in the minibus, and Bill nodded.

'Whatever you can think of that represents a land of the darkest imaginable shadow of death. Perhaps the worst of it was that, along with the colours, the sounds disappeared, too.'

Bill paused, and for a moment we all sat listening to the hum of the minibus motor.

'People always talk about the silence you get in the forests, but that silence is made up of thousands of little sounds. Birds singing and rustling in the trees and on the ground; the sound of a wallaby munching the grass somewhere in the distance; insects buzzing and beetles waddling across the leaves; worms crawling around in the soil; the hush of the wind in the grass and the bracken, the leaves and the branches. But out here in the Grampians it was like you'd walked into a soundproof room. It was utter deathly silence.'

Bill flicked on the indicator and turned left towards the B160 highway. We would drive around Otway far to the north.

'Don't get me wrong. I still think this is the greatest country on earth, but sometimes you can't help thinking that . . .' – he gave another cough – '. . . that people, us humans, we're just swarming parasites on Mother Earth's skin, tickling and teasing, irritating and provoking her until the only thing she can do is disinfect herself. She whips up a fever, and it probably hurts like jumping into a bath of acid, but at least it does the trick. She's just got to do it.'

JYRKI

And I couldn't help thinking about the same thing happening in the north: a fever rising, the snowline retreating, the glaciers melting. As the winters become warmer, people's livelihoods will disappear.

Lapland is being raped right now just like Australia was in the past. Giant hotels, more and more new skiing resorts, shopping centres, health spas. Come and enjoy the untouched nature of Lapland!

All common sense has been lost. Every day at the Rabid Reindeer we arranged enormous buffets for the guests. The majority of the food was brought in by lorry or aeroplane. Every day the food that wasn't eaten — and there was plenty of it — ended up in the rubbish bins, ladled off serving trays, bowls and plates left on the tables and into giant black bin-liners by the kilo, by the tonne.

Now it'll all be spewing methane somewhere.

At some point things will come full circle.

I remember descending the Col du Palet Pass in the French Alps. After days spent surrounded by untouched natural landscapes I was so shocked that it hurt.

Maybe during the winter season Val Claret is a real picture-postcard landscape of snow, dark-blue skies and continual Christmas lights. But during the summer months seeing the place is like listening to nails scraping down a blackboard. Do these slalom hotshots have any idea what their skiing hellhole looks like during the summer?

The mountainsides have been skinned alive, so much so that their immune system is now irreparably compromised. The whole valley is now a persistent sore on the landscape. I couldn't help imagining what it would look like in another ten years' time: the bottom of the valley would be nothing but a bed of gravel, furrowed by the occasional trickle of water and dappled with a few brave tufts of grass. From amid the deserted wastelands, roofs, chimneys, the upper storeys of tall buildings would sprout. The twisted, rusted remains of cable-car pillars would protrude from the moraine slopes like the half-buried bones of dinosaurs.

Once the snow starts coming down as rain – something that is happening more and more at this altitude – tourists will vote with their feet. The waters of the melting Grande Motte glacier and the endless rainfall would continually push soil and earth down the slopes, hoed bare by the bulldozers, and before long nobody would want to prevent or slow down the inevitable decline and fall of the Val Claret.

They're red and dotted around the place. When you take care of the glass and turn the switch it starts ringing in every room, so loud your skull rattles.

People look at one another thinking this must be some mistake, soon there'll be somebody on the Tannoy telling everyone to chill out. But when there's no announcement they start shifting restlessly and whispering and nudging each other. Then the idea of smoke and burning gases pops into their heads, that and the image of everyone uncontrollably barging their way out of the doors, shoving people, falling over, trampling on each other.

And then that's exactly what happens.

If it's a kiddies' showing, Mummy's and Daddy's sleeves will soon be covered in snot. Are we going to die? they ask, bawling. And all the while there's the ear-splitting sound of the alarm, PRRRRRRRRRRR, that'll eventually strip their nerve endings raw.

SOUTH COAST TRACK, TASMANIA
Louisa River
Thursday, March 2007

HEIDI

On the banks of the brook, on both sides near the path openings, the under-growth has been worn away and the ground is covered with nothing but a carpet of eucalyptus leaves. I can only begin to imagine how merciful the shade of a large tree must feel after crossing Southy from the other direction across the scorched plains of buttongrass. Louisa River is fairly wide and deep, and even the sound of the flowing water has a cooling effect. But we are damp and dirty, and I'm shivering – still.

I can't see anyone else, and I think to myself that other people are hardly likely to turn up as it must be pretty late already, but as I shrug off my ruck-sack by the bottom of a tree Jyrki looks at his watch and his expression softens and brightens.

'Eight and a half hours! Bloody hell, we *are* a pair of *troopers*.'

Eight and a half hours. So it can't be much more than four o'clock.

Even Jyrki sheds his rucksack and eyes up potential spots beneath the trees. 'What about over there?' he says, pointing to a fairly level clearing further along the brook where it looks as though there are tree trunks to sit on.

'I'm going to get out of these boots first.' Without waiting for Jyrki's response – he never takes his boots off until we've set up camp – I sit down on the tree root and start unlacing my Meindls. Right enough, you could wring water from the hiking sock on the right foot. And I wring it tight, and a fair amount of lukewarm dirty water dribbles between my fingers. My thin liner sock has changed colour and now features a brown print of my heel, my toes and the ball of my foot.

I remove the insoles of both boots and put them out to air. I'm well aware that the boots won't even be close to dry by morning. If I had some newspaper there might have been some hope. I can't waste my pamphlets on this. And we can't make a fire.

I put on my Crocs and walk off after Jyrki. He's standing in a larger clearing, big enough for a couple of tents, and points to a comfortable-looking bed of leaves between the trees. 'That looks like a good spot – but if there are lots of people on their way we might get some neighbours.'

'Does it matter?' I ask, and Jyrki starts to explain something about once camping near someone who snored like a road drill, but I'm not listening any more, because I can see something.

It's small and transparent and curved, and it has a blue screw top.

The wombat bottle.

It's lying on its side on the ground, half covered by the bushes, and its inner surface is covered in a thin film of condensation, like a bottle that has been empty for some time.

'Very funny. Very mature. A real masterclass in growing too attached to inanimate objects,' I say and kick the bottle.

When Jyrki turns towards me, a look of confusion on his face, and sees the bottle, to my surprise his expression doesn't change to that of a mischievous little boy who had just played a really good trick but to one of genuine astonishment, almost shock.

I pick the bottle up from the ground, but my voice is no longer as angry and accusatory as before because there's something so wrong with his reaction. But the words still come out the same.

'I mean, where the fuck has this suddenly sprung from? Your pocket?'

Jyrki lifts up one of his hands as if to hold me off as I shake the bottle in front of his face. 'I don't understand. I really don't understand. If you dropped it when we were leaving Deadman's . . . someone could have picked it up, brought it out here then got tired of carrying it.'

'Nobody at Deadman's was going the same direction as us.'

'Well, they could have arrived after we went to bed.'

'And left before we woke up? No, when we woke up it was still dark. Nobody in their right mind would set off for Ironbound in the dark. Besides, you can't exactly avoid noticing other people on that path. Jesus, I mean, if someone's overtaken us they'd have had to fly.'

Jyrki's mouth opens.

'So you might as well own up,' I continue, slightly unsure of the situation, as Jyrki still seems genuinely baffled.

Suddenly he grabs the bottle and thrusts it close to his face. 'How do you know this is even the same bottle? It's a Qantas freebie, for crying out loud. Everyone travelling to Tasmania flies with Qantas. Every other person must realize a quarter-litre bottle might be handy on the road.' Jyrki is laughing now, relieved.

'The label on this one is torn off in the same way,' I say, a little helplessly.

By now a mocking tone has crept into his voice. 'Right, as if the label doesn't eventually fall off every bottle that gets held under water on a regular enough basis. Labels don't tend to tear off in particularly individual and creative ways. And look at those scratches. Did your bottle have scratches like that?'

I lean my head forwards and look. Fair enough, I don't remember the couple of lengthwise scratches. It's as if this one's been scraped across the stones at the bottom of a creek or handled by something sharp.

'Still, it's quite a coincidence,' I say, my voice now somewhat subdued.

It seems to me I am trying to tell you a dream — making a vain attempt, because no relation of a dream can convey the dream-sensation, that commingling of absurdity, surprise, and bewilderment in a tremor of struggling revolt, that notion of being captured by the incredible which is of the very essence of dreams . . .

— Joseph Conrad, *Heart of Darkness*

OVERLAND TRACK, TASMANIA
Narcissus Bay
March 2007

HEIDI

I could see my breath in the air at Narcissus Hut. Wearing a pair of thermal tights I'd bought in Te Anau, made partially from possum wool, and three layers of clothes, I gingerly clambered out of my sleeping-bag. Last night the temperature had clearly dropped below freezing. It would probably have been much warmer in the tent than on these chilly bunks. But the first time we wanted to erect the tent all the decent spots had been taken. It's a good thing we were sleeping on the upper berth – you'd think the lads downstairs would give off at least a little warm air.

My bladder had reached bursting point; I absolutely had to get up. I pulled my hiking trousers over my possum pants and wrapped my coat around my neck as a fourth layer, shoved my feet into my hiking boots; I couldn't be bothered to tie them up but stuffed the laces beneath the tongue. The duck-boards led down to the outdoor loo, which, like all the toilets at Overland, had been built on a set of supporting poles like the most regal of thrones. And the throne wasn't occupied! Hallelujah!

In my coat pocket I found what was left of a packet of tissues. What luxury it is to be able to pee *and* wipe. Crouching in the bushes, no matter how much you did the cha-cha-cha on your haunches, a few drops always made their way on to your panties, and after a few days they really started to whiff.

When I stepped outside I saw that the clouds had broken and for a moment the sun lit up the misty slopes of Mount Byron, gilding them, and it felt as though I were looking at their dew-soaked, untouched glory only a few minutes after their very creation. *Morning in Tasmania*. I was witnessing daybreak in Tasmania. Those ordinary words felt suddenly real, so real that I felt butterflies at the bottom of my stomach.

At the same time I was vaguely amused, having a 24-carat aesthetic awakening on the way to the bog, surrounded by the smell of human shit.

*

Overland Track was the most famous and most popular trail in Tasmania. It was like the Great Walks in New Zealand – in high season it can be impossible to get on it because there are only a certain number of berths along the route. Thankfully luck was on our side. When we arrived in Melbourne, Jyrki went straight online and found a starting date with four free spaces left. A few clicks of the mouse and a few hundreds dollars later we had ourselves a hiking licence.

We caught the bus as soon as we got off the Spirit of Tasmania, and the journey to our starting point at Cradle Mountain took just over two hours.

Overland was majestic and wonderful, of course, but all the while I could see a strange undefined fire burning in Jyrki. Desolation and untouched nature, the dizzying scenery, the incredible purity of the air – it had everything. But it also had organized group hikes for people with matching hats and water flagons covered in adverts; it had purpose-built paths; it had huts kitted out with all mod cons; recommended daily legs that were sensible to the point of humiliation. All the while Overland was hinting, whispering to us: this virgin island has so much more to it, somewhere further on, something purer and more innocent, untamed by restrictions, regulations and unnecessary mollycoddling.

It was a bit like if I was Overland, and while we were dancing together Jyrki was always looking over my shoulder, somewhere into the far corner of the room, where a more appealing woman, even more tailor-made for him, was gyrating seductively. And I would have that stinging feeling of not being enough for him because there's always something wilder, something more mysterious elsewhere. In the arms of a man who can't appreciate the jewel he's got – and Jyrki always wants what he can't have – what he's holding tight to his chest at that moment just isn't enough.

Back in the cabin Jyrki had set up the stove, and the water in the pot was almost boiling. Our bag of food flaunted its emptiness, but it didn't matter because in an hour's time we'd take a boat to Cynthia Bay, where we'd be able to get some proper food. And then the bus back to Hobart.

Jyrki was chatting to Jonas, a Swedish guy, who was telling him all about some trail along the southern coast. Jyrki's eyes lit up.

'South Coast Track? There was something in our guidebook about that.' Mike, an older man in the cabin who had entertained us every night by criticizing other people's equipment, joined the conversation.

'Compared to South Coast Track, Overland is a walk in the park. Southy is where you can really show what you're made of.'

Our water came to the boil, and I interrupted Jyrki, who by now was pretty excited. I took a sachet of instant coffee and two small muesli bars from our food bag. It was all we had left. We stirred our coffee and opened up the muesli bars.

Jonas looked first at us, then our bars, then us.

'Is that your breakfast?'

We nodded.

Jonas shook his head. 'I've always known you Finns were tough, but I didn't know you were *this* tough.'

Jyrki burst into a happy laughter, so happy that the syrupy oat flakes almost flew from his mouth. He was the one who had calculated our food for Overland. To the gram.

The brat is pulling toffee popcorn out of a giant bag, stuffing it into his gob in great heaped handfuls. He'd cram it into his face with both his fat little paws if he didn't need one of them to hold the bag. He's giving it a go, though, squeezing the sack against his chest with one chubby arm and shovelling the light-brown clumps in behind his teeth, holding the other arm crooked like a spastic. He can't even be bothered to chew properly; his cheeks and the tops of his gums are bulging, and while he's chomping away a mixture of spit and toffee with white crumbs swimming in it dribbles out of the corners of his mouth.

The shiny rustling bag is made of slippery material, and the kid's hold on it is just awkward enough. Mummy is looking through the shop window at a dress that'll never fit her as I walk past and jerk my knee. I knock the little punk right in the back. His arms flail in shock, and the bag flies into the air in a magnificent curve, popcorn falling across the shitty street like snow churned out beneath a plough.

I'm already a few metres away, lighting up a smoke. By now the sprog's howling so much his head might explode, and the remains of the toffee popcorn in his mouth are spilling out over his chin and down his front. His voice cuts through everything; it's better than a fire alarm. Passers-by turn to gawp as the kid leans his head back and bawls, wails, yells his lungs inside out until he's purple in the face.

Mum stares helplessly at the goodies strewn across the pavement, then looks at her little urchin's snotty, twisted face.

'Dear oh dear, how did you manage to do that?' she simpers.

The brat crouches down and tries to scrape up the popcorn from the street, but Mum grabs his arm and yanks him up, setting off another wave of screeching from the little shit's slimy popcorn-filled mouth.

'Don't cry, dear. Let's go and buy you some ice cream,' Mum gibbers, and the kid shuts up in a flash as if someone had switched the off button.

'A ginormous ice cream,' the obnoxious offspring says.

'Any kind you like,' replies Mum and leads the metre-tall monkey to the nearest place that will dispense some instant carb-comfort. A flock of pigeons and sparrows has gathered around the spilt sugar bomb on the street, picking at it frantically with their beaks, their eyes glancing sneakily to the sides as they gobble up their sweet treat.

SOUTH COAST TRACK, TASMANIA
Louisa River
Thursday, March 2007

JYRKI

You shouldn't really wash your clothes in the creeks, but Louisa River is large with plenty of flowing water, and she's not using soap, so I turn a blind eye as she rinses her socks. She hangs them on the branches of nearby trees and tries to find a spot along the riverbank still bathed in the rays of the setting sun.

As I cook some food, she sits mending the seam of her trousers with duct tape, cack-handed endearingly.

It'll soon be dusk.

I use the wombat bottle as a tooth mug. I rinse my toothbrush and hand her the bottle.

When she starts brushing her teeth I ask her for some paper, tell her I'm going for a pit stop. She raises her eyebrows: either she hasn't understood or she thinks the use of motoring terminology is strange and out of place for someone who enjoys spending time surrounded by nature. She mumbles something incomprehensible with the toothbrush in her mouth and digs around in her pocket, and instead of a packet of tissues she hands me a yellowy-brown sheet of paper.

I stare at it. A religious pamphlet.

She shrugs her shoulders. She removes the toothbrush from her mouth, and, squinting, says if I think this is neither the time nor the place for blasphemy, I can wipe my arse with a stone.

HEIDI

When the terrain is nothing but mud and rock faces, with no prospect of a break in sight, no real rivers to cross but only paths running with water that you have to negotiate, you forget to drink enough. You forget to drink when it's snowing, and it's not the least bit warm; you don't remember that your body is losing fluids all the time, even though you're freezing your tits off in the wind.

Dehydration has built a nest in my head, rhythmically pecking and scratching away behind my temples.

Apart from falling over on the pavement and grazing my knee as a kid, the greatest physical torment I've endured as an adult has come in the form of hangovers and the occasional bout of period pain.

Compared with this, the minor muscle aches I had experienced after our first stretches at Queen Charlotte seem positively enjoyable. I remember asking Jyrki if he had any painkillers. He said he was saving them in case we seriously sprained anything. Used in the right place, they could make or break the whole trip.

When Jyrki comes into the tent I turn on to my side and face away from him. If I had wings, I'd wrap my head deep inside them and spend a moment breathing in my own comforting cosily stuffy scent.

JYRKI

After sleeping in the overcrowded peak-season cabins in New Zealand you might think that moving into the tent would create an altogether new sense of intimacy – there we would lie, in the cosy, tight green embrace of the tent walls, in our very own space, warmed only by our very own breath and the glow of our very own body heat.

I imagined it would be easy and natural to turn to her, kiss her, slowly undo the zip on her sleeping-bag or gently stop her as she's getting ready for bed. Put my hand on her naked back and move it higher and higher; caress her cropped hair, press my lips against her neck.

How come it's so damn easy when we meet up for the first time in two weeks, but it's so difficult now?

Maybe it's because there just isn't time for things like romance in a routine like this. We haven't agreed on the logistics, and there's no space here for improvisation. How can you undress seductively when there isn't even enough room to kneel up properly?

And what about the practical side of it? Soon there would be blotchy secretions all over the sleeping-bags and the silken bag liners. Every last piece of textile we have with us has some other important function, too. And imagine getting up in the middle of the night to wash downstairs with a mug and some cold stream water.

But she wouldn't say no. She's never said no – to anything.

At first I thought she was one of those rare women who don't use their pussy as a bargaining chip. But as time went on I realized that her cheerfully consenting to anything and everything was something even craftier: if you never give the other person reason to feel unsatisfied you end up wielding even greater power.

Just thinking about this causes unavoidable action in my trousers. It's been a while, because you can't exactly get down to business in berth accommodation. I have to put the guidebook to one side, curl up next to her and kiss her ear. She smells faintly of sweat and strongly of woman.

She mutters something indistinct. I can hear floating tears echoing around her sinuses.

I tell her I just wanted to say goodnight.

She utters an almost inaudible goodnight.

The forest around us clicks and crackles.

There's no initiation either into such mysteries. He has to live in the midst of the incomprehensible, which is also detestable. And it has a fascination, too, that goes to work upon him. The fascination of the abomination — you know. Imagine the growing regrets, the longing to escape, the powerless disgust, the surrender, the hate.

— Joseph Conrad, *Heart of Darkness*

HOBART, TASMANIA
February/March, 2007

JYRKI

Even though the Moo lager I had in the pub at the Lark Distillery micro-brewery was the best beer I had tasted since arriving in Australia, I was still pissed off. Big time.

She asked me why I was so down in the dumps.

I showed her the guidebook. South Coast Track looked like a hell of a trip, I said, but there was one fundamental problem with it. If we wanted to get there we'd have to fly.

I showed her the rough map in the book. As the name suggested, the route wound its way along the southern Tasmanian coastline with a couple of diversions deep inland. One end of the track was at Cockle Creek, the south-ernmost point in Tasmania – and the whole of Australia – that could be reached by car. The other end was in a place called Melaleuca, eighty-six kilo-metres to the west. Melaleuca had a few trekkers' cabins and a bird-watching station, but there was no road link whatsoever. It did have a runway – the story goes that a light aircraft once had to make an emergency landing there, and the only way to get the thing out again was to clear enough space for an airstrip.

If you wanted to start at Cockle Creek, which was at least reachable by bus from Hobart, the only way to get from Melaleuca back to civilization was to fly or to trek back the way you came. It would have been madness to try to hike there and back – I can't think of anything more boring that covering ground you've already seen but backwards. Repetitive stretches of the journey become even more mind-numbing if you already know how boring they're going to be. Dangerous and exhilarating spots are no longer any kind of challenge but are simply a nuisance because all the excitement has gone. It doesn't take long before your motivation drops below freezing.

However, if you wanted to start from Melaleuca the only option was to fly there.

I cursed the arseholes that come up with these sorts of schemes.

She offered to pay, thinking it was just a question of money. She was always waving her traveller's cheques around every time we talked about making decisions, as if money were the answer to everything.

I told her I wasn't planning on burning any more fuel, given the amount I'd already burnt in getting here.

I felt hot, and I had ants in my pants every time I thought about the route. I'd gone online to find out more about it. Back at the tourist information centre in Hobart National Park I had bought a map of South Coast Track. It was no joke: the path really was in the middle of nowhere, just like Jonas and Mike had told us at Overland.

She looked at me quizzically.

I said that at Narcissus Bay I had decided that Overland would be the last time I ever went out on a route that was designed for amateurs crawling in ten-kilometre legs. I reminded her that all the guidebooks and tourist leaflets had split Overland's sixty-five kilometres into six one-day hikes. We covered it in four, and we would have done it in two or three if the cabins had been sited a bit more sensibly along the route and if bus timetables had been coordinated with our plans.

I read her a section from the *Great Walks of Tasmania* leaflet: *This is a coast where one's place in the universe is never in doubt. Money, position, education and status don't count and don't help.*

She asked me whether I thought South Coast Track was going to be terribly difficult.

I told her it was recommended for experienced trekkers and that there were a couple of people around this table who met that description.

She shrugged her shoulders uncertainly.

Fuck it.

At least out there we wouldn't bump into any more hen parties.

I took a deep swig of Moo and opened out the map of Tasmania again, as if staring at the southern coastline would offer some kind of solution.

HEIDI

Johnny Cash's 'Ring of Fire' was playing in the background.

Jyrki was flustered and talking non-stop; in his excitement he had forgotten all about his pint as he scribbled notes in his jotter of squared paper. He had found a faint line of dots on the map, leaving Melaleuca and heading roughly to the north-east; it was a four- or five-day route, an extension of South Coast Track. This route, Old Port Davey Track, seemed to run through areas even more remote than the main route and looked as though it ended up where no man has boldly gone before. OK, it appeared to meet up with some kind of dirt track, but even that was still a good few hours' arduous drive from civilization. A Tassielink minibus operates a service between Hobart and the Scott's Peak end of the track three times a week. That way we wouldn't have to get a flight, and we wouldn't have to double-back on ourselves. Jyrki had already fallen in love with his plan.

It felt so silly. Here we were, in Tasmania, an island no larger than Ireland, and we were about to become more isolated from civilization than you could ever get in Finland, no matter how remote a place you found in Lapland. Except maybe if you got lost around the Russian border area.

Jyrki was talking like a man possessed, his overly long limbs thrashing around. He was sure, he had decided, he had found an extra sugar coating to the enthusiasm that Jonas and Mike had planted in him at Overland. He was already calculating the number of days these two combined tracks would take; he counted how many hours it would take per day and stared at the contours on the map in the hope that they might give him some idea of the route's degree of difficulty. The trek from Cockle Creek to Scott's Peak would apparently take us about ten days.

I asked him whether it might be smarter to trek the opposite direction, to start at Scott's Peak and make our way towards Melaleuca and from there onwards towards civilization, to Cockle Creek — how much nicer it would be to end up somewhere with other people and some traffic. But that wouldn't do, that simply wouldn't do, because we only had a finite number of days left down under, and we had to use them cost-effectively, and as there would be a bus from Hobart to Cockle Creek tomorrow morning, why wait? Now we had to buy food and ask about getting seats on a suitable return bus.

But because this is Jyrki we're talking about, that really meant only *asking* about seats, not actually reserving them. Jyrki found out that some seats had already been booked on the buses leaving around the time we should be arriving in Scott's Peak, which meant the bus would definitely be running.

'They won't leave paying customers in the middle of the woods,' he said. 'It's too big a risk to book seats and pay for them in advance, then end up missing the bus because of some unforeseen change to our schedule. If that happens, you'll never get your money back. If we know the bus is running we can always get a ticket from the driver; we'll always be able to get away. It might mean sitting on the floor of the bus for a few hours, but so be it.'

'Ring of Fire' started blaring out of the speakers once again. The tape loop in this pub must only have been about ten minutes long. It was as if the same obsessive bird had taken flight, singing at the top of its lungs in an attempt to protect its territory once again.

I was still at school back then; it was a while ago. The bus stop was on a slight slope. Snow was packed hard across the surface of the road. You could see the bus's skid marks in the snow. The tyre tracks were hard and shining, and if you slid back and forth along it with your shoes it soon felt smooth and frictionless.

Sprinkled some fresh snow on top.

The bus arrived and the driver braked. Jesus, you should've seen the way it lost control, sliding and swerving at speed towards the embankment of snow. Like watching a mammoth keeling over.

This one comes to mind quite often. Nobody thinks about what's hidden somewhere out of sight. Nobody knows which packet of porridge oats has a needle pushed in through the seam, or where exactly the shards of glass are buried in the kiddies' sandpit.

Nobody can see.

If I kick a white stick out of your hand, it's your own fault for being blind.

JYRKI

As I'm taking down the tent the next morning I see that the left guy rope at the back of the tent is dangling loose. The rope and its knot are lying casually on the carpet of leaves.

She must have pushed the tent peg in too deep when we put the tent up last night; the loop of rope has managed to come away from the hook. I've shown her a hundred times how you're supposed to leave the tent peg sticking out between one and one and a half centimetres above the ground, then it's at the right angle to make sure that the guy rope is taut and stays in place. Either that or she stepped on it when she went for a piss. The peg has been pushed into the ground, and the rope has come loose.

I ask her.

She says she hasn't trampled on any of the hooks.

I let out a few uncontrolled buggerations. First of all, they're called tent pegs, I say, and now this particular one is stuck in the ground.

By pulling the guy rope tight and holding it to the ground at slightly different angles, I try to find the spot where the tent peg must have sunk into the earth. The layer of dried leaves and detritus on the ground is pretty thick. I brush the rustling scrub to one side, but I still can't see the tent peg.

If it's gone in so far that we can't even see the top; we'll never find it.

She doesn't seem to appreciate that tent pegs are equipment. You don't go around losing them.

She claims she put the tent peg at the agreed height and asks whether we couldn't make a replacement peg out of wood. Then we could buy a new one at the Mountain Design store once we're back in Hobart.

I ask her whether she's ever seen the heavy, cumbersome lumps of metal they sell as tent pegs around here. Hilleberg's pegs are light and compact: aluminium, European, smart.

Really. A wooden peg.

Eventually I'm forced to admit that I packed a spare peg. But only one, and that's why this can't happen again.

She nods with that bloody-minded look on her face, as if she genuinely doesn't understand what's really important.

HEIDI

When I crouch down for a morning piss I notice something.

I pull a piece of pamphlet from my pocket, soften it for a minute by rubbing it between my fingers and gently press it between my legs.

When it comes back into my field of vision it's a reddish colour – or what was the biblical term? *Though your sins be as scarlet.*

Great. I knew this would happen.

JYRKI

Ironbound is still impressive when we see it in the Tasmanian dawn. The hillside rises up behind us high up into the sky. On the bare rock face there is a clear diagonal line, so thin it could almost have been drawn with a stick of chalk: the path we came down yesterday.

Compared with yesterday's trek, today's path feels ridiculously easy, nothing but duckboards across the damp, even clumps of buttongrass; the same plain, reaching as far as the eye can see, that we saw as we were coming down Ironbound.

She starts talking about gaiters again; they wouldn't have been completely redundant on Ironbound. I don't say anything. Then she thinks about how the word is pronounced. Imagine sending someone off to buy some gaiters, she starts explaining, and they came back wearing a couple of alligators on their feet.

I can't help but laugh. It's like something straight out of a Gary Larson cartoon.

I tell her I've always wanted to come up with a computer game that's really violent. It would be set in Australia, and its name would be 'Combat Wombat'.

She laughs.

We can still feel the previous day. It's lurking cold beneath our skin. You can tell because we're babbling like idiots.

After yesterday's exertion the even, undulating terrain here is a real treat. Now that we don't have to spend all our time concentrating on our every step, the air is full of our incessant chit-chat and jokes that are abysmally bad but that, for that same reason, seem just right.

I have time to watch how she walks: full of energy, warmed up and finding the rhythm in her step.

Christ. She's just crossed Ironbound, and there she is striding across the duckboards, one hiking boot marching in front of the other and trying to look serious as she witters on about some stupid wannabe wallaby story, and something inside me is deeply moved.

Ironbound was something that had to be shared. Nothing would have been the same if we hadn't shared it, without knowing every step of the way that another pair of eyes and ears, another group of muscles, was sensing the same as I was; knowing that at any moment you could pull Southy out from between her ears like a box of treasure that only we could open. And, boy, how she'd already shared it. She'd come out here, her body almost entirely untrained, the reach of her limbs so much shorter than mine, without the benefit of a year in the army, with almost zero experience. And not once had I sensed that she was about to sit down on the nearest tree stump and say, 'Listen, Jyrki, I've fucking had it. I'm never putting on this sticky shirt again, heavy with grime and stiff with spots of salty sweat. I want a foamy bath, a litre of perfumed moisturizing cream and a Greek salad, or I'm going to scream.'

I look at her, and I'm filled from head to toe with a strange rush of warmth. I imagine it wouldn't be an altogether stupid idea to share paths with her from now on – always.

I almost say it out loud.

But I don't.

Not yet.

Somebody called Louisa had clearly made a big impression on the guy who originally charted this region. After setting off from Louisa River, the most significant place in the Louisa Plains crossing is – wait for it – Louisa Creek.

The creek is wild. The climb down into the gorge is a challenge in itself. There are only a few tree roots and rocks protruding from the embankment to offer you a foothold. The embankment itself is nothing but sheets of almost vertical rusty-brown soil. The force of the current in the river has carved out the gorge, making it steep and deep. You can clearly see how much water has rushed through here during the rainy months.

A ten-metre length of rope has been stretched across the creek. It's at just the right height so you can grab hold of it if you reach your hands up. Holding on to the rope, you can wade through the water even when the river is slightly fuller. It would probably serve as a decent support if the water level were below waist height. If the creek were completely full, the surface of the water would cover the head of even a tall man; if it came up to your chest, the current would inevitably knock you off your feet. Now there's just enough water flowing across the shadowy riverbed that you can cross with relative ease, jumping across the rocks.

It's no wonder that crossing these rivers during the flooding season is 'forbidden' – meaning that guidebooks tell you not to try your luck. Lots of people probably do.

I would.

I'd take her over with me; I'd snatch her away so that the bubbling water wouldn't even realize it was being cheated.

This place is a designated campsite, too. There are worn patches on both sides of the river beneath the trees. It's no surprise really: people are forced to wait here, often for days at a time.

We fetch water from the creek as it trickles tamely by.

HEIDI

We clamber out of the bush and on to the beach only to discover the cove is adorned with a large rubbish dump: pieces of rope, plastic bottles, metal cans, chunks of polystyrene, plastic bags, floats.

I pick up a rusty spray can. It used to contain shaving-foam. I look over at Jyrki, whose cheeks are now covered with uneven stubble. His face reacts to the sight of all this trash, but he doesn't say a thing.

'Look, this must have belonged to someone who swears by the virtues of being clean-shaven in all circumstances.'

'It wasn't a person that brought it here; it was the sea.'

I glance at the heaps of garbage. True, it will all float.

'In the Pacific Ocean there's a floe of rubbish twice the size of the USA, and it's made up of exactly this kind of stuff,' he says kicking a faded red plastic canister. 'Ten metres thick, a hundred million tonnes of shit that smothers a million birds every year – and a few sea mammals for good measure.'

For a moment I'm utterly speechless. 'Why does nobody do anything about it then?'

'Because no matter who you ask about it, it's always someone else's problem.'

'Oh. But why hasn't this been cleared up? I mean, this would be easy to get rid of. You could take it by boat to Cockle Creek.'

Jyrki looks up at me from a bowed position; he's taking off his hiking boots for the last few kilometres along the sandy beach.

'Because if you clear up someone else's rubbish then people really will start leaving their shit behind them. It would be proof that your refuse will always magically transmogrify into someone else's problem.'

JYRKI

To my left the foaming, turquoise sea soothes the eyes. My toes dig into the sand. After days encased inside my hiking boots they are jumping for joy.

In the sand I can see a frayed piece of orange plastic rope. It makes me think of the dumping ground in the Pacific and the heaps of rubbish at Buoy Creek. Appropriately enough, there were plenty of garishly coloured buoys among the rubbish. Against the gentle colours of the Tasmanian landscape, they were like a slap in the face.

It's mildly amusing to think of the innocent young first-time trekker girl we met in the first cabin at Overland who had packed a bag full of tinned food, bananas and apples, then came up to us old-timers, her head tilted to one side and both hands filled with rubbish, and asked where she should dispose of it.

It's as if every piece of information about every national park, every document, hadn't already made it perfectly clear time after time. Everything you bring with you when you arrive – that means *everything* – you take with you when you leave. Everything, every last sweet wrapper, every eggshell. The fact that some rubbish will eventually decompose is still no excuse for throwing it where it doesn't belong. A strip of orange peel soaked in preservatives will catch your eye in the bushes for years to come. If you want to wipe when you go into the bushes for a piss, you pick up the paper and take it with you. The same goes for a used condom, a chewed piece of gum or a cigarette end. It's a good job you're not allowed to start an open fire in national parks, because

146

then people would try to burn aluminium foil and even empty gas cylinders as well as any paper and plastic shit they might have. I've seen burnt remains like this before. How come people are strong enough to carry all manner of containers into the park when they're full but suddenly haven't got the strength to carry them away once they're empty?

Back in New Zealand, when we registered at Kepler, in addition to various papers and receipts we were given a bright-yellow resealable plastic bag with instructions printed on the side about how to deal with your rubbish. So there wasn't even the old excuse of not knowing where to put your junk when you wanted to wash your hands of it.

That's it: it's all about washing our hands. What would we do if nobody ever took care of our rubbish? How shocked we are when someone tells us to deal with it ourselves. Producing refuse is as natural as breathing. And it's just as natural that this refuse is always Someone Else's Problem. It's with this kind of logic that people dump washing-machines and fridge carcasses in the woods and by the side of the road, because eventually someone else will have to remove them to stop them being an eyesore.

Lay-bys are full of people's construction waste, months' worth of rubbish from the summer cottage and old redundant furniture. A skinned deer was even dumped in one.

Try collecting every strip of salami skin, the paper casing of every sticking plaster. Try flattening every empty tin of tuna, dripping in oil, so that it's more convenient to carry. It's a no-brainer that you take everything out of its double packaging, get rid of all cardboard boxes, clingfilm and plastic biscuit trays before you leave and make them someone else's problem in the rubbish bins at the hostel or the local supermarket, wondering why on earth people ever needed these things in the first place.

And although we'd all been given the same resealable rubbish bags at Kepler we had only got as far as the picnic area on the first day's leg before we noticed empty tins of sardines and chocolate wrappers left in the outdoor toilet. They had been neatly left in the corner of the hut, as if a diligent cleaner with rubber gloves comes past to collect them every day. Westerners' brains are clearly programmed with the strong conviction that public toilets clean themselves.

Every person on this earth should be forced to collect all the rubbish they produce in a week and pile it in a heap on the living-room floor. You wouldn't be allowed to take it away; it would have to be there all week. And for once it wouldn't be Someone Else's Problem.

And there, don't you see? Your strength comes in, the faith in your ability for the digging of unostentatious holes to bury the stuff in — your power of devotion, not to yourself, but to an obscure, back-breaking business.

— Joseph Conrad, *Heart of Darkness*

JYRKI

She was holding a packet of chocolate biscuits in her hand, inching it closer to the shopping basket, looking at me all the while.

I shook my head.

She said they were rich in oats and fibre as well as chocolate. Then she said that it would be nice to reward ourselves after a hard day or with our morning cup of tea. That you always need carbohydrates. And fibre.

Gently but firmly I took the packet from her hand and replaced it on the shelf. We already had enough to carry.

Our shopping trolley contained enough food for two people for ten days:

8 wholewheat flatbreads (diameter *c.* 20 centimetres)
1 packet of rice and maize cakes (12 cakes)
16 slices of pepperoni
10 slices of processed cheese
4 bags of instant mashed potato powder
2 packets of tuna (chunks)
500 grams orzo pasta
1 tube of tomato purée
1 large onion
1 small bulb of garlic
250 grams length of salami
4 packets of instant noodles
2 packets of powdered soup
20 muesli bars
1 bag of dried apricots
1 tub of smoked almonds

In addition, we were already carrying four meat stock cubes, twelve tea bags, six sachets of instant coffee, ten packets of sugar we had pinched from the aeroplane and various cafés, a couple of sachets of salt and a camera-film tub filled with mixed spices.

I had decided ages ago that there was no point investing in those obscenely expensive packets of freeze-dried trekking food. With these ingredients we would be able to cook varied nourishing meals. And they'd fit into a much smaller space.

The rewards on this trip were going to come from something else altogether.

HEIDI

I'd never been really that hungry on any of our previous treks. Food had been more of a ritual than a necessity; it was a way of passing time. If you were especially tired, you almost had to force yourself to eat. But I wanted those cookies.

I was standing in the middle of the shopping aisle at Woolworths with my arms firmly crossed.

'I'll carry them.'

'We share all the carrying. If you take them, I'll have to take something else.'

'They don't weigh very much.'

'But my rucksack is already heavier than yours.'

'Well, I suppose that's because you're bigger. It's not my fault your clothes are larger and heavier and your sleeping-mat weighs an extra four hundred grams because it's full length and –'

'It's unfair to bring biology into this; that's something we can't do anything about.'

'Is this about money? Those muesli bars you chose are cheap store-brand stuff. I'll pay for the cookies.'

'Because those so-called sports bars cost about three dollars each. We haven't come all the way out here for fine dining. And, besides, if we get really hungry you women have extra stores of body fat.'

JYRKI

Eventually I had to ask her who had taken charge of the shopping for Overland. Was there ever a more skilful demonstration of effective food rationing?

On that matter she found it pretty hard to return service. She looked at me for a moment and thrust the cookies back on to the shelf. OK, she said and added that we still needed a couple of things from the toiletries department.

Plasters, I thought, and gave a nod.

HEIDI

Jyrki must surely know that women have periods – in the past he must surely have had had direct contact with the phenomenon – but his brow furrowed when he saw me throwing the packet of Always Ultra into the shopping trolley.

'You do understand where it is we're going?'

I looked at him the way you look at someone who opens their mouth in completely the wrong situation only to state the blindingly obvious.

'South Coast Track.'

'*And* Old Port Davey Track.' Jyrki picked up the packet; its cosy softness almost disappeared inside his enormous fist. 'And how exactly are you planning on disposing of these once they've been used?'

'Well . . . you know, the way you . . . the normal way . . .' The mere mention of the subject made me blush. People just don't *talk* about these things.

'The normal way?'

I thought of all the instructions there had been at Overland Track, and it started to dawn on me.

'There are some pit toilets, but only as far as Melaleuca. And anyway, you don't put *anything* in a pit toilet that isn't biodegradable. These have got God knows how many layers of protective plastic.'

I stared at him and realized that the furrow between my eyebrows must have vaguely resembled a double Grand Canyon.

'Sooo?'

'After use – that is, when you want to get rid of them, assuming you don't want to carry them around with you – you'll have to open up the towel, take a stick or something and scrape out the absorbent padding, the cotton wool or cellulose or whatever it is, into the pit toilet. Then you'll have to roll up the non-biodegradable parts into a tight package. Aren't these supposed to have some kind of wrapper with a strip of sticky tape? You could use that. The package will be about the size of a cigarette. Then you keep them in a resealable bag. And as for all that plastic packaging that's another matter altogether . . .'

A look of nothing but utter seriousness radiated from Jyrki's face. I grabbed the pack of towels and threw it back on the shelf then snatched a much smaller box of tampons and brandished it in front of his face.

'What about these?'

'Hmm, I suppose they're OK. They don't have any of those applicators. But all that cellophane . . . And once they've been used you can't leave those anywhere either, no matter how much cotton is in them. OK, the box is made of cardboard, but you can dispose of that here.'

'And what about the used ones?'

'You carry your own refuse.'

I dropped the box of o.b. tampons into the trolley.

Jyrki didn't know that I also had a couple of panty liners in my rucksack, but this wasn't the moment to get into a discussion about them, too.

I remember one of my classmates who had decided to start having children in her twenties. On one of her rare nights off, she and I went out for a couple of ciders together. Suvi told me how guilty she felt about the volume of nappies she got through with her children. She had been told that disposable nappies were the work of the devil. Under no circumstances should people use them because they create plastic, shitty Mount Everests at dumpsites up and down the country. But when she'd thought of switching to terry nappies, she had serious doubts after learning about the effect on the environment of 90-degree white washes and the quantities of phosphates in all that washing powder. On top of that, there was the question of whether it was better to let a child become traumatized by walking around in soggy cotton nappies versus letting them get so used to being in ultra-absorbent Pampers that they would never see the point of learning to use a toilet. And imagine what fun it must be for the kid starting school with a bag of spare nappies. She rounded off her outburst by concluding that the most ecological solution was to feed the offspring to the neighbours' huskies at the first convenient opportunity.

It made me shudder to think that I had once fantasized about starting a family with Jyrki.

The best place to dump stolen bundles is in the toilets at restaurants or department stores. A bus has got to be pretty empty, so nobody notices you just walking off. Sometimes a park bench or the top of a bin will do nicely.

When you take the target out of its pram you've got to do it quickly but not in a rush. So it looks like you're the kid's parent or some family member. Then walk away. Stay cool.

It's a pretty big deal. The brat might start screaming, and that always attracts unwanted attention.

Ante says the fuss that breaks out over these things is in a league of its own. We're not just talking about a runaway dog here.

Dogs are easier. Still, they can find their own way home. Sometimes. Depends what we've got in mind for them.

HEIDI

Cox Bight is a miniature paradise.

From the sands at the shore it's only a half-metre step up to the embankment, covered with short velvety grass.

The campsite is situated right next to the beach, sheltered by the trees and bushes. This is clearly more worn away and in more regular use than any of the other campsites after South Cape Rivulet. This place is evidently visited by far more people, but that doesn't mean that the spot isn't lovely and idyllic. Apparently the leg from Melaleuca out here is a day's walk and seems every bit as popular as the stretch from Cockle Creek to Rivulet. That means tomorrow's leg will be an easy stretch with a decent path. To one side, a small distance from the shore, where the path leads off towards the pit toilet, there is even a small, roofed information hut, not quite big enough for someone to fit inside. More of a small stand with a registration book.

Or, rather, there should be. Now all that's left of it is a pile of charred remains. The ring-binding has survived along with the soot-edged stubs of pages a couple of centimetres in from the spine. Someone clearly got a kick out of torching this. Perhaps it was the same person who had scraped away at one of the booth's legs with a knife and singed it with something like a cigarette lighter. The idea was presumably to bring some excitement to a leisurely Sunday-afternoon walk.

'They're determined, I'll give them that. First the flight from Melaleuca, then a thirteen-kilometre walk just to vandalize something that's vitally important to other people,' says Jyrki.

So yet again we can't register ourselves.

A little way further into the campsite there are a few clusters of tents, all people trekking in the opposite direction. The fact that we're from Finland always causes surprise; all the others are Aussies from the mainland. They find it amusing that we've come here to enjoy the heat: for them Tasmania is a cool spot where they can escape the 40-degree heat back home. They ask us about Ironbound, and we tell them that it certainly lives up to its reputation.

Jyrki shows them his crippled hiking pole like an old war wound. I don't bother pointing out my thighs, my shins and my arms. Anyone with a pair of eyes can see the blotchy leopard-skinned pattern covering them. The variegated bruises of different shapes and sizes are interspersed with nasty-looking scabs and scratches that I picked up yesterday before pulling on my hiking trousers. The *magnum opus* is in the middle of my right thigh, a bruise the size of my palm, blue in the middle and edged with a pretty yellow coloration, making some of it look a distinct shade of green.

As we chat with the trekkers heading east, I can see Jyrki's back straightening – without his even noticing it – and with that same expression of fake indifference, the same nonchalant shrug of the shoulders that was all over the body language of the guys we'd seen at Cockle Creek who had already crossed Southy.

JYRKI

I splash myself with water straight from the small brook. Further downstream there's only the beach and the sea, so it's fine to wash myself here. No point lugging water up to the campsite, and for once there's no need to be frugal with it.

Once I've towelled myself off and started pulling on my civvies I hear a rumble. I look up.

This weather front can't be coming in across the sea, from the Antarctic, the way they normally come. If it were coming in from the sea, we'd be able to see it a long way off. This one is coming from behind the forested horizon, from the west-north-west. This is a freak air current, a weather phenomenon that's becoming all the more common across the globe.

I grab my hiking clothes and the wombat bottle, which I've been using to scoop up washing water. I stick my feet into my Crocs and make my way straight towards the campsite. The tent is a few hundred metres to the west of the brook.

Just then I feel the first raindrops.

HEIDI

I'm convinced I left it on that tree trunk. Absolutely convinced.

There were still about half the slices of pepperoni left in their opened vacuum pack. I was supposed to cut them into strips with the Swiss Army knife and mix them with the mashed potatoes. I had been keeping a beady eye on the water we're heating up – because we mustn't, mustn't, *mustn't* waste any of the gas in the cylinder – and I'd gone back into the tent, for a minute at most, to change my panty liner for a tampon then come straight back out to sit on the tree trunk and use my body to shelter the cooker from the strengthening wind coming in from the sea.

And now the pepperoni has vanished.

Could it have been the wind?

My eyes scan the surrounding scrub.

I sigh with relief: the wind. It's been gaining in strength all the while; by now it's pretty blustery, and the sea is white with the crests of waves. The plastic pepperoni packet is flapping in the wind a few metres away at the foot of a bush. It's flown a good distance.

I take a few steps and pick up the packet.

It's empty.

I crouch down in a panic, run my hands through the grass and undergrowth, my eyes darting across the ground looking for something round and a browny-red colour.

I can understand the packet being blown away, but I can't see how the slices of pepperoni – tightly packed together and sealed with fat almost into a single chunk of meat – could have been picked up by a gust of wind if it had rolled out of the packing.

Possums are timid and only move around at night.

Rats?

I stop for a moment, frozen. It's as though I can see myself, I can almost smell the pepperoni – cumin, peppers, magnificent animal fat. I can remember – and the more I think about it the more real it seems – how my hand could have reached up towards my mouth, as if by magic, how my teeth could have sunk into the slices of sausage; the thought of my molars squeezing the dizzyingly salty, spicy meat juices on to my tongue . . .

'No,' I hear myself saying, but my tongue is still twisting around inside my mouth, searching for the taste of pepperoni and strips of meat, and I fall to my knees once again.

'Please be here, please be here, please be here,' I chant out loud, crawling in increasingly large circles between the bush and the tent.

Right then I hear a boom of thunder.

The raindrops are so large and heavy that they soak you right through, leaving spots the size of coins on your clothes.

Our rucksacks are lying open beside the tent, open bags of clothes and supplies carelessly hanging out of the loosened drawstrings. The food bag is open, too, propped up beside the tree trunk we've been using as a kitchen.

I jump to my feet, forgetting all about the pepperoni, and take wide running steps.

I unzip the vestibule and the mosquito net and hurl first one open rucksack in on top of the beds then the other. Then the bag of food, my sarong – still damp – all the socks, shorts, T-shirts hanging on a nearby branch, then a quick glance towards the cooker, which is now hissing angrily with each raindrop that strikes it. I turn off the gas supply and plonk the pot into the vestibule along with the cooker. Finally I dive inside behind everything else.

By now the rain is now drumming on the roof of the tent.

I can hear the sound of heavy footsteps and panting, then Jyrki comes crashing into the tent, almost uprooting the guy ropes in the process. It's chaos inside the tent: our damp rucksacks, the two of us half soaked, the bundle of trekking clothes in Jyrki's hand dotted with droplets of rain. I hurriedly zip up the doors at the entrance.

The rain is coming down like a roaring wall.

It's coming down so hard that grit and loose sand is being splashed halfway up the tent's outer walls; from the inside of the tent it looks black and grainy. Jyrki tries to find a comfortable position. He can't: rucksacks and bags and clothes fill the space. I could never have imagined that, compared with this, normal life in the tent feels quite spacious. We're literally drowning in stuff.

'Those have to be packed up and put in the vestibule.'

Jyrki starts shoving things into his rucksack. Not in his typical systematic fashion; the main thing is that everything is inside. He is ready long before me and opens up the inner zips.

Water is running through the vestibule. The ground simply can't absorb a flash flood like this, and now water is flowing in under the vestibule walls which aren't attached to the ground. The gas cylinder with the cooker on top and the kettle are like small crags in a flooded river. For once Jyrki is speechless. His hand falls limply against his rucksack.

'What about the rucksack covers?' I suggest.

'They might keep the rain out, but the water will get through if they have to swim in this. Then, in no time, it'll have soaked through to the stuff at the bottom of the rucksack.'

'But isn't everything in plastic bags or those waterproof things?'

Jyrki shakes his head. 'Imagine what those rucksacks will weigh tomorrow if they suck up water all night. Then they'll be wet on the inside, the DrySacks will be wet on the outside, and the plastic bags won't keep anything dry. At least the tent's waterproof.' He zips up the vestibule and we look at each other for a moment, both leaning against a rucksack the size of our upper bodies. 'Let's try and stack them over there, on their sides against the walls at the foot of the tent. We can sleep with our legs together.'

I nod.

We try to hang the dampest of our clothes from the guy rope running along the inside of the tent's roof, forming a curtain between us.

And with that we are in separate rooms, in a space no bigger than three square metres.

The air is so thick I feel like I could suffocate.

JYRKI

Once it's almost dark and the adrenalin in my blood has dropped off a bit it occurs to me that we haven't eaten anything.

From the other side of the makeshift sarong-and-T-shirt curtain she says that the cooking water didn't have a chance to heat up properly.

I clamber to my knees and peer into the vestibule. The ground is nothing but mud. All the food we'd put aside for dinner needs boiling water. I suggest we cook dinner inside the vestibule. The mashed potato will be ready in no time, and we can mix in some strips of sliced pepperoni.

She panics at the thought. Surely you can't light a fire beneath a roof of nylon fabric. Candles can set fire to things very high up, she says. Isn't nylon fabric highly flammable?

I tell her I've cooked inside the vestibule before, and that some people even use the cooker inside the tent itself, although I wouldn't go that far.

She's clearly worried – and with good reason. People die in tent fires, and losing or damaging the tent in these conditions would hardly be the ideal scenario.

Still, it's annoying that she doesn't trust me. But, on the other hand, it's a fair point that we need to conserve our gas.

We've still got flatbread and rice cakes, she says. And cheese.

I point out that we've been saving them for breakfast and suggest pepperoni and dried apricots instead.

She is quiet for a moment then says she's not really hungry, adding that the last thing she'd want to eat is those sour, sugary apricots because she can't imagine how she could go outside to brush her teeth in these conditions.

I listen to the incessant rush of the rain, like a waterfall drumming on the tent. The storm front seems to have been caught right above Ironbound. It doesn't look like it's going to be over any time soon.

I think about the sweet, sticky layer the apricots leave in your mouth. Perhaps we should have picked up some xylitol chewing gum after all. Then I remember that nuts neutralize the pH levels in your mouth.

She gives an indifferent response of sorts. We eat smoked almonds. I count out fourteen and a half per person.

We had a stroke of luck, I tell her. Judging by the volume of the rain, anyone looking for the ultimate extreme experience will be sure to find it trying to cross Louisa Creek tomorrow.

HEIDI

We're lying inside the tent, in the deep darkness.

I can't move my legs; they're wedged between Jyrki's legs and one of the rucksacks. The air is so moist that it sticks to my fingers.

The storm is still rumbling with no sign of letting up. Although I've closed my eyes I can still sense the bolts of lightning forcing their way beneath my eyelids like flat needles.

Then I hear it.

It starts quietly, but it's getting louder all the time. It's like an approaching squadron of fighter jets moving in behind the drone of the rain and the howl of the wind. At times it fades a little, but each time it grows the roar is even more penetrating than before. The trees are rustling and wailing in the forest around us. Every now and then I can hear something large, heavy and rotten falling or dropping to the ground with a crash.

I let out a quiet cry. The bottom of my stomach is aching with fear, my heart's racing at a million kilometres an hour. The raging sea is far too close; I imagine it would only take a second for it to breach the half-metre embankment separating us from the beach. The creaking trees, crying out in agony, are right next to us, above us, ready to topple.

Tears squeeze their way out from the corners of my eyes. I can't control my loud gulps of breath.

A hand reaches out from under the curtain hanging between us. Jyrki's arm comes to rest on my chest, wraps itself around me, pulls me and my sleeping-bag tight against him.

'Hey. It's only the tide.'

By now I'm sobbing – long, heaving, spasmodic sobs – because I know at some point I'm going to have to tell him I've lost the pepperoni.

JYRKI

Heidi's cousin and her fiancé, both our age, not even thirty, were swept away by the tsunami at Khao Lak.

I can understand her overreaction.

I've got to do something. She clings on to me in the darkness.

I whisper comforting nonsense into her ears. With my body I protect her from the roaring, rushing wall that she thinks is rising up from behind the horizon.

There were moments when one's past came back to one, as it will sometimes when you have not a moment to spare to yourself; but it came in the shape of an unrestful and noisy dream, remembered with wonder amongst the overwhelming realities of this strange world of plants, and water, and silence.

— Joseph Conrad, *Heart of Darkness*

SOUTH COAST TRACK, TASMANIA
Cox Bight to Melaleuca
Saturday, March 2007

JYRKI

It's incredible how much a thin piece of nylon fabric that doesn't even absorb water can weigh once it's wet. As we roll up the tent, no matter how much we try to shake it, it seems to have doubled in mass.

The morning is chilly and bright and beautiful. The droplets of water blown off the eucalyptus trees by occasional gusts of wind and the muddy earth under foot are the only reminders of the storm.

My night of insomnia stings my eyes and lingers as a stuffy taste in my mouth. I'm shivering a bit from lack of sleep and the moisture hanging in the air. She pulls on her hiking trousers; I'll make do with shorts.

As I'm boiling up some water to make a cup of tea, she suggests we might as well have some soup for breakfast.

I'm startled. Packet soups aren't meant for breakfast.

Well. I suppose it is a fact that we barely had any dinner yesterday.

She hands me a packet of soup so quickly that she must have been holding it out ready.

HEIDI

I'm spooning chicken soup into my mouth when I notice something black on my arm.

After a storm like that all kinds of crap falls out of the trees. I flick at it with my free hand, but it won't come off my skin. Then I see it swelling at one end and stretching itself out into a funnel.

I give a shriek and start flapping and shaking and swiping at my arm, but the black blob won't come off.

Jyrki reacts, then sees something moving on his thigh, too, albeit on top of his shorts.

'Leeches. Well, well.'

'Get it off! Get it *off!*' I shout.

I don't even know why I'm so supremely revolted by the thought of having a parasite on me, sucking my blood, my vitality, eating away at me, and I can't even bring myself to look at my arm as Jyrki, after flicking his own leech to the ground, starts prising the thing off my skin, a thing that's slimy and shapeless.

'I should have remembered this,' says Jyrki. 'These little buggers drop down from the trees after its been raining. We should check each other's necks every now and then before we reach open ground.'

JYRKI

One of our colleagues packing up his stuff has heard the scream and comes over to see what all the fuss is about. I explain that the little lady wasn't exactly enamoured with our invertebrate friends. The bloke chuckles and hangs around for a chat. He'd set out from Melaleuca the day before, and he's clearly more than a bit impressed when he hears we're continuing along Old Port Davey Track. He asks about our food packages waiting at Melaleuca.

My surprise is tangible. He notices this and continues, explaining that the few people that take our route or that trek back and forth along Southy usually have extra supplies flown out to Melaleuca beforehand. You call the flight operator. You put together a packet of food and take it to the airport. All this costs a nominal freight charge because the plane takes travellers out this way almost every day, so it's a handy way of shipping out extra provisions for your group. Then halfway along the track you can stock up your rucksack with fresh supplies that you haven't had to break your back carrying all the way.

I glance to one side. She seems to be concentrating on pressing a piece of paper on to the spot where the leech bit her.

I quickly change the subject and wish the guy good luck for Ironbound. He says his goodbyes and walks off.

Hopefully the food-package conversation didn't fall on the wrong set of ears. If she's overheard him I'll never hear the end of it.

HEIDI

After a two-hour hike the sun is so high in the sky that I've absolutely got to take off some of my clothes. I don't bother listening to Jyrki muttering, as if to himself, that it would save time if certain people could make their minds up about this sort of thing back at the camp.

I sit down on my rucksack and take off my boots, then my hiking trousers with their duct-tape seam. I stand up and start pulling up my shorts when Jyrki clears his throat. Meaningfully.

'Erm, hang on,' he says, pointing vaguely towards the back of my knee. 'Hang on a minute.'

I look down and this time the scream gets stuck in my throat, comes out as nothing more than a shrill little squeak, and I feel almost faint.

At the back of my knee there is something black and shiny, fat and greedy. It's like a pulsating boil, the length and size of half a finger.

I can't sit down again. I can't bend my knee. The mere thought of the surrounding skin coming into contact with it is enough to make my hands quiver.

'It must have jumped down from the trees this morning before you pulled on your trousers,' says Jyrki. 'And you wouldn't have noticed it. Where's the food?'

Food? What, are we going to stop for a snack? But Jyrki is already undoing my rucksack and rummaging around for the bag of food. He finds the resealable bag with the small sachets of salt and pepper that we'd pinched from the flight. He rips open a sachet of salt.

'Stretch out your leg.'

I straighten the leech leg out behind me, and I feel an almost stupid sense of relief, as though I'm pushing the disgusting creature further away, even though it's still attached to me. Jyrki sprinkles salt on the bend in my knee.

'What are you doing?' I'm ashamed of the shrillness in my voice.

'This might just be an old wives' tale, but leeches apparently don't like salt. Should make it easier to pull it off.'

As Jyrki pulls the leech off my leg, I can't feel anything. Not a nip, not even the repulsive sensation of it pulling away. Jyrki disposes of the thing in his hand.

'Why didn't it hurt?'

'These little guys release an anaesthetic into their victims and an agent that stops the blood clotting. Speaking of which, that's bleeding quite a bit. There are thick veins behind your knee really close to the surface of the skin.'

'It'll have to be bandaged with gauze and skin tape.' My voice gradually returns to normal, because even I can do this. 'The first-aid stuff is in the left-hand side pocket.'

A ruby-red stream of blood is trickling down my calf as if, diverted by the tampon, my period had tried to find an alternative way out of my body.

JYRKI

Two blokes walk towards us with surfboards under their arms.

Bloody hell, how much fuel has had to be burnt to transport all that out here?

They approach us on the path as if this is something they do every day. Little bags on their backs and their man-sized fibreglass toys supported against their hips.

As if everything I've been trying to escape has overtaken me, jumped out from behind a corner and slapped me in the face.

They acknowledge us casually and disappear around the bend in the path. I have to consult the map: sure enough, a little way back there's an almost invisible trail leading away from the main path. It winds its way down to a virginal cove that these guys must have heard people bragging about. They absolutely had to see it for themselves, had to surf the waves that other people hadn't yet polluted with their presence.

Still, you've got to admire them for carrying stuff all that way. It's a thirty-kilometre round trip from here to Melaleuca. Thirty kilometres with a surfboard beneath your arm, just so you can tell your mates you've surfed at Hidden Bay.

HEIDI

After crossing the gentle shoulder of a series of hills I can see the Melaleuca lagoon in the distance, a primitive, sandy airstrip and the buildings standing next to it, and the sense of relief almost makes me burst into tears.

Buildings themselves don't mean anything – they're not shops, they're not refreshment stands – but a building is still a building. It doesn't let the rain in, you don't have to lie there with your legs bent uncomfortably across your rucksack, the wind doesn't rattle the walls, and if a eucalyptus tree falls on the roof the person inside won't necessarily be crushed to death.

Buildings also generally feature real toilets, ones with walls and something to sit on. At this point in time that's more than enough. I don't care how much it smells, as long as my arse is high enough above the slurry of excrement heaving with innumerable life forms.

And where there are buildings there are generally other people, too. Real people. Members of the same species, not just occasional passers-by or people that happen to be sharing our campsite but representatives of a certain level of civilization. Real people, people who stay in the same place for more than a moment, people you can ask all kinds of things you could never ask fellow competitors in the never-ending how-far-out-into-the-bush-have-you-been contest. The most you ever ask these other competitors is how swollen or dry a particular river is, because everybody's basic assumption is that they already know everything.

Perhaps once again, although it's just for a moment, we can feel like part of a group, a community, feel that somebody else might shoulder some of the shared responsibility for one another. If Jyrki were suddenly to collapse with a brain haemorrhage I wouldn't have to panic all by myself, to flap around and try to do something. I'd be able to find other people to take control of the situation. People who know better, people who know what they're doing.

What's more, this place has that blessed little sandy airstrip. With the help of that airstrip, it's only an hour from here to the heart of a more civilized civilization than we could ever dream of demanding. So if Jyrki did have that brain haemorrhage – just a minor one, of course, but he'd be unconscious for a while and need immediate treatment – or if I tripped on the duckboards and sprained my ankle just badly enough, then we wouldn't be in too much trouble. If there's a runway there must be working links to the rest of the world, and if you have money and credit cards and a communication link to civilization it's almost as if you're already there. The rest is just a matter of sorting things out. But if your foot slips out in the middle of some God-forsaken place like Ironbound, or if a tidal wave smashes you against the rocks at Granite Beach, or if you're out in the bush – of which there is plenty in Southy – and step on a venomous snake (and there are plenty of them, too), then you're basically dead. Although in theory – and I really mean *in theory* – you'd still have hours to live.

As the buildings grow larger and larger I become more and more excited. Here there are even two huts. No need for all that obsessive palaver of the tent; here we can spread out and relax on a bunk. You can cook food sitting on a real bench; you can eat at a real table. Someone might have left an old magazine or a frayed paperback in the hut. The very thought of having something to read brings water to the virtual mouth in my brain.

We've hiked like the wind. After leaving the coast there was a slight incline, but the path has been so good and dry and easy that it's only midday, and it would appear that the rest of the path up to Melaleuca runs along duckboards. A lazy afternoon – I mean a real lazy afternoon with something civilized to do – opens out in front of me like the Holy Grail.

I can't help smiling as we reach the edge of the runway. There's a water tank by the side of the airstrip building. That feels like civilization, too; this is a place where you don't have to drink from brown murky ditches. Here you can drink from something built by human hands.

JYRKI

I start filling the Platypus with water from the tank, careful not to let any go to waste. Well, after last night's generous downpour the tank should be full again.

Although we're over ten kilometres away from the actual coast, the lagoon at Melaleuca, even though it's far inland, is connected via a narrow sound to Bathurst Harbour, a vast inland body of water that joins the sea to the west. This waterway has enabled people to ship in machines and equipment by boat, to maintain the old tin mines and this cluster of buildings in Melaleuca. I'm surprised there aren't any old tractors rusting away in the bushes.

She's eyeing the narrow dirt track that leads towards a bird-watching shack partially hidden in the bushes and from there on to the huts. They look like they're made of corrugated iron. Yuck.

It's still very early, and the weather's good. Old Port Davey Track runs across the airstrip and winds off to the west. I remember that according to the map it crosses a river then continues north-west through an easy-looking flat section of terrain. It then reaches Joan Point where you have to cross to Bathurst Narrows by boat. You can't spend the night there; there's no drinking water. Across the sound at Farrell Point there's a brook and a designated campsite.

I take another look at my watch. Another four, five hours and we'll have reached the crossing.

I ask her why she isn't filling her water bottles.

She looks at me as though I've just crawled out from beneath a stone.

I tell her we've got plenty of time to reach Farrell.

She pauses for a long moment. Then she asks what we're going to do with the extra day. Weren't we supposed to arrive at Scott's Peak on Thursday?

167

I remind her that there's a suitable bus connection leaving Scott's Peak on Tuesday, too.

She asks why we're suddenly cutting two whole days out of our agreed timetable. I can hear from her voice that she's retreating further and further into her dug-out, assuming defensive positions.

I show her the day-leg suggestions on the other side of the map. Although the leg from Farrell Point to Watershed Camp is split across two days, it's only twenty-four kilometres. For us that's barely a day's walk.

Her jaw hits the floor. She's about to say something, but I continue now that I'm in my stride.

From Louisa River to Cox Bight was eighteen kilometres, I remind her. We covered that in six hours, and this terrain looks pretty similar. Mathematically that means twenty-four kilometres should take us eight hours. That's an average day's stretch. So if we just behave ourselves and carry on now we'll cover the two-day stretch tomorrow, and what do you know — we'll be in Scott's Peak on Tuesday.

HEIDI

I look at the buildings in Melaleuca, only a tantalizing stone's throw away. At the same time I realize that if we follow Jyrki's new plan we can be out of here two days ahead of schedule.

I think about Ironbound. I think about it for a long time. Then the previous horrendous sticky night, the flooding Rivulet, the steep incline at Granite Beach. I think about the leeches, the pit toilet at Deadman's Bay, and it all makes me shudder. I think of Ironbound once again, and the shuddering continues. I think about the endless — can it really have taken us only six hours? — trudging across the tussocks and bogs on the plains after leaving Louisa River and the lung-wrenching climb across Red Hill, which Jyrki seemed to think was a piece of cake. Cox Bight, which was like a tiny little paradise before the snake of the thunderstorm appeared and ruined everything.

I think of my back and my shoulders.

I think of my period.

I think of walls and roofs.

I think of Tuesday and Thursday.

I think of Forneaux Lodge and Punga Cove back at Queen Charlotte Track. This is like leaving Forneaux Lodge without the promise of Punga Cove.

And while we're on the subject of New Zealand and Sabine Circuit and Granite Beach, how many times has Jyrki said, as if in passing, that this was nothing, nothing at all, we might as well do another ten-kilometre stretch now that we've warmed up properly?

I've had enough. I won't hear a single 'If you managed that, you'll manage this, too,' comment ever again.

I look at Jyrki.

He looks weird with a week's worth of stubble, and his hair, instead of being carefully shaven, is now a short crop the colour of the dirt track.

'Can't we even go and have lunch in one of the huts?'

Jyrki sighs and glances at his watch for the umpteenth time. For someone so thrilled about living rough his attachment to his watch is unhealthy, to say the least. He slings his rucksack over his shoulder, and we stride off along the crunching gravel road.

The corrugated iron hut is, well, made of corrugated iron, and the air inside is hot and stuffy, but still it feels like walking into a hotel. The first thing I see is the kitchen work surface with a shelf above it. On the shelf people had left a few boxes of matches, several half-burnt candles and . . .

Half a dozen different-sized gas cylinders.

It makes sense. People have ended up with leftover gas that they don't want to take on to the aeroplane. Or for some reason they might have simply wanted to lighten their load. Either that or they haven't seen the sense in carrying a half-empty gas cylinder all the way home when someone else could use it.

My eyes dart around the hut like a guppy. A couple of sleeping-bags and rucksacks have been laid out on the bunks, but there's plenty of room. People starting out along Southy tomorrow; people waiting for the plane home; bird-watchers. You could count them on one hand. Yee-haa!

On the table there's an old small-format magazine, *Natural History Digest*. Small print but something to read all the same. And great paper. There's only one crumpled scrap of the religious pamphlets left in the side pocket of my rucksack.

I take another look at the gas cylinders. Their combined contents, even if there's nothing more than a fart in each of them, represents eight whole minutes of free cooking time at the very least. Cooking time in a place where the wind and the rain cannot, *cannot* reach the cooker's flame.

And that's not all, I realize. We could even afford to heat up a pot of water and have a decent wash, pour something almost body temperature over our necks and heads and backs.

I lower my rucksack to the floor and make a mental note of which bunk I'm going to have. The one up there on the left looks good enough.

'So I suppose we should take the boat across to Bathurst Narrows today then?'

My voice is steady and business-like, my PR skills coming to the fore. Jyrki nods. He seems not to know whether to be happy about my knowledge of the route or worried about my tone of voice.

'I mean, we should make sure we set aside enough time. You never know what could happen. It's a much longer crossing than the one at Prion Beach, and the channel is probably much deeper. What if the wind whips up or there's a storm? What if there's a problem with the boat or we arrive there and find there's no boat at all? We need to leave ourselves some leeway. If there's no drinking water at Joan Point, what are we going to do if we're still stuck there by sunset? Think of how quickly the weather turned yesterday.'

I look at Jyrki with large calculating eyes.

'We could make ourselves a proper meal. Look!' I gasp and gesture towards the row of gas cylinders as if I'd only just seen them. 'We could boil up some of that pasta.'

I know I'm really close to winning him over. He's the one who bought the orzo in his great wisdom.

'And we could visit the bird-watching hut and see if we can spot the famous rare orange-arsed parrots the guidebooks were raving about. It's not every day you get to see super-endangered orange-arsed parrots.' I almost squeal, because now's the time to put the icing on the cake, now's the time to play it up, to bring home the victory.

Jyrki sniffs.

'It's the orange-*bellied* parrot. *Neophema chrysogaster*.'

How does anyone know stuff like that?

Jyrki shrugs his shoulders. 'I suppose we do need to let the tent dry out.'

JYRKI

For once people and buildings don't necessarily mean that someone's trying to make a quick profit.

When the weather's bad and planes are delayed, people waiting for a return flight can sometimes find themselves with absolutely nothing to eat. Even though they've got walls to protect them and a roof above their heads. Even though there are dozens of people in the same place, that doesn't automatically translate into shops and kiosks.

Everybody out here has a carefully calculated amount of food with them. If somebody who'd missed their flight because of yesterday's storm came in here and asked for a rice cake, I wouldn't be able to give him one. If he offered me a hundred dollars, I couldn't sell.

Out here I might as well use banknotes to wipe my arse instead of those pamphlets.

There would be something poetic about that.

The cooker is hissing on full blast. The gas cylinder is twice as big as ours, and it must have about a quarter of its contents left. Let it cook away.

This is going to be a banquet. First a handful of shredded salami to grease the bottom of the pot. Then plenty of garlic and some chopped onion. Sauté it for a moment, stirring occasionally. Then fill the pot with water and add a meat stock cube. Once it's dissolved, add a cup of orzo and a good squirt of tomato purée. Then sprinkle with mixed spices from the film tube.

The smell is quite dizzying.

While we're waiting for everything to cook, she brings in the hut's registration log. The log is large and hardbacked, different from the lame squared-paper jotters we'd found in the past. She leafs through the book, laughing at some of the comments and looking for any mentions of Finland. When she can't find any she convinces me to write down our names and our projected timetable for the trip to Scott's Peak, so that we will go down in history as perhaps the first Finns to travel along this trail.

The first pot of food disappears from our plates as we're waiting for the next one to cook. We only slow down once we're on the second plateful.

We lick our plates.

We afford ourselves the luxury of warming some water for the dishes. We take care of the washing-up a good distance into the bushes behind the hut, making sure not to leave any grain of pasta or sliver of onion on the ground. The water, smelling slightly of salt, tomato and fat, soaks into the earth.

The magazine on the table has disappeared. I see a corner of it jutting out from beneath a sleeping-bag laid out on the upper bunk.

There's still a shitload of daylight left.

HEIDI

According to the log in the bird-watching shack, the last person to visit this place sat on his arse for six hours without catching sight of a single orange one.

Deny King Memorial Hide is a surprisingly large wooden building in the middle of the bushes; it must be over fifteen square metres in size. One of its walls is half made of glass, and beneath the observation wall someone has built a shelf of some sort, a work surface where people can set up tripods and other bird-watching paraphernalia. On the other wall there's a slanting shelf bearing the observation log, and the walls themselves are covered with aged photographs of different birds and their names. I look around for a photograph of the orange-arsed parrot – I wouldn't know what it looked like otherwise. *Neophema chrysogaster*. It's a spectacular looking creature with splashes of pure turquoise on its beak and wings. Then, true enough, right between its legs is a rusty orange blob, as though the bird, too, was having its period.

Jyrki is, of course, watching the feeding spot like a hawk. Now that we're here I drop hints that it's really important for him to see one of these chicks.

He protests, saying a shack like this isn't the real way to spot rare birds. They must be being fed, if not overtly then in secret. Jyrki probably thinks that if you pamper a threatened winged creature too much, sooner or later it'll rise up against its keepers, and before you know it all local species of parrot will gather on the roofs of Melaleuca and start attacking unsuspecting hikers' rice cakes in some great Hitchcockian scene.

As Jyrki presses his nose up against the glass I notice a small space, separated off from the rest of the shack, with a screen and containing a table and a couple of chairs, presumably a place where people can eat their sandwiches while waiting their turn or having a break from staring into the camera finder.

Hang on a minute. A space to have lunch.

There's one particular item in the room that I allow to take shape in my consciousness, something that's almost too familiar to notice, except when it's something you haven't seen for a while. For weeks. Ages.

'Bloody hell. Bloody hell!' I hear Jyrki hissing. 'That's it!'

I look at his hand as he scoops the air, come over here, quickly, and I just about manage to tear my eyes away from something far more interesting.

To hell with the orange arses.

'Kea: The Open-Programme Bird'
by Jiselle Ruby and Anthony Verloc

During the time of the Gondwana continent, over eighty million years ago, New Zealand was part of a mainland whose closest neighbours were Eastern Australia and part of what is now the Antarctic. When Gondwana split up through the forces of continental drift, many entire ecosystems of trees and animals moved with the sailing landmasses. Certain forest types common in New Zealand have also been found in Chile and Tasmania. To this day, despite the considerable distance, Australia and New Zealand share around 80 per cent of their most highly evolved flora.

SOUTH COAST TRACK, TASMANIA
Melaleuca
Sunday, March 2007

JYRKI

It's odd waking up in Melaleuca — no whispering or murmuring of the trees around us, no waves lapping against the shore in the background as though they were keeping count of our heartbeats.

At night you could hear the drone of the mosquitoes. We never had any trouble with them in the tent, as long as you remembered to open the mosquito net only when absolutely necessary. Here it only takes your hut-mates to pop out for a slash in the night. Especially coming back into the hut, once the mosquitoes have picked up the scent of their victim, the opening and closing of the door brings in a legion of bloodsuckers every time.

The leg ahead of us will only take a few measly hours. It feels strange and wrong. We've got used to waking up before sunrise, drinking tea as day breaks and being on the road by seven o'clock. We've woken up to the sound of bird-song and the gradually strengthening light filtering in through the tent wall.

It's half past seven. I stretch and laze in my sleeping-bag. The bunk is harder than the ground, usually softened with layers of eucalyptus leaves. My sides ache despite the sleeping-bag and the mat.

Wow, she's awake. She's already taken the breakfast stuff out and is now boiling up some water. Not using our gas cylinder, of course, but one of those left on the shelf. She's learning.

My nostrils are filled with the smell of instant coffee. Coffee! Again, she hasn't even bothered asking me.

She walks up to the bunk with her coffee cup in one hand and our gas cylinder in the other hand. She holds it out towards me and asks whether we should pack one of the leftover cylinders from the shelf as well, just in case.

I shake the cylinder and weigh it in my hand. It feels like it's still half full.

We're not going to start lugging another two hundred grams of metal around just for fifty grams of liquid gas, I tell her. She nods and slurps her coffee, happy as a lark.

HEIDI

'Go and fill up the water bottles. I'm going to pop back there one last time.'

We've carried our rucksacks out to the fork in the path near the bird-watching shack. I point in that direction.

'What for?'

'Just want to see whether there have been any more sightings of the orange arses.'

Jyrki's brow sets in a furrow, but he can't say anything. He was so chuffed and excited about our two-second sighting of the orange bums that I'm sure he'd be pleased to know that nobody else has seen them since. Besides, filling the water bottles takes time, and you don't need two people to do it.

The observatory is quiet. Nobody around at the moment. Good. On the other hand, I would have done this no matter who else had been around.

I got everything ready back at the hut while Jyrki was checking whether the tent was dry. It's a good job my shorts have such large cargo pockets.

In the corner of the observatory shack there is a real *bona fide* rubbish bin.

There they fly, happily, carefree, straight into the pale-green plastic bucket lined with a black bin-liner. In go the thin plastic fruit bag stuffed with the empty remnants of a sachet of noodles, the used teabags, the plastic processed-cheese wrappers, tin foil that had once contained tuna, packets of instant mash, tissues (used to clean plates and knives) that we couldn't reuse in the pit toilets, even the greasy plastic wrapper from the missing pepperoni sausage. And in goes the resealable bag with three used tampons lying next to one another like dark, fat, carmine red caterpillars, and alongside them a couple of brown-stained panty liners complete with their backing papers rolled into tight little spirals.

Goodbye, farewell, *auf Wiedersehen*, adieu to the muesli-bar wrappers floating at the bottom of my pocket, the chewing-gum wrappers, the remains of a couple of plasters, their protective papers and bits pulled off my skin. The cotton wool bandage and the skin tape from the back of my knee.

This is a magic receptacle where rubbish disappears by itself and travels far out into a distant universe.

I feel a hundred times lighter as I all but dance out on to the path along-side the runway.

JYRKI

This airport terminal is just a shack, completely open on one side and with a couple of wooden benches – nothing but a glorified bus shelter. There's a guy with a dark beard in his thirties sitting there with a rucksack waiting for the day's plane. Tied to the side of the rucksack is a robust-looking tripod. Next to him on the ground is a large aluminium camera case.

I say hello. The guy starts chatting straight away. A clear case of extreme social deprivation, so clear that I can't help smiling. Even without all the photography equipment, his chubby, tidy appearance reveals he's not one of our hiking colleagues.

The guy is from the USA, out here on a research grant to photograph birds in the wild for a book. He excitedly tells me how, in his whole life in the States, he's spotted about three hundred different species, and in five weeks in Australia he's spotted the same number again. Tasmania is his final stop before flying home.

I ask him whether he's seen the orange-bellied parrot. He claims he has, at the observatory of course. But he seems far more excited about a different sighting altogether. A nocturnal species, one he hasn't yet been able to identify. It's not the *Pezoporus occidentalis*, apparently, which is only found in mainland Australia. But it can't be the *Pezoporus wallicus* either, which is a local species that moves around during the day. I remember my friend Juha Lehtinen, the most enthusiastic amateur ornithologist I know, mentioning that one. The ground parrot is an especially rare bird, and it's name states the obvious about its nesting habits. This means these birds are directly affected by bush fires, too. I can't recall whether they suffer because of them or benefit from them. There was plenty of information on Australian parrot species on the internet. I couldn't avoid it when I was looking for the Finnish name for the orange bellies. Just to make sure. Now I've seen one I can drop it into a conversation with Juha and tell him in passing that there are barely two hundred of them in the world.

I hear the crunch of footsteps. I look behind me. She's coming out of the observatory and raises her hand in an exaggerated wave to our photographer friend. Without saying a word she starts stuffing the newly filled water bottles into her rucksack pockets.

The photographer carries on with his incessant chit-chat. There are still lots of deserted areas of Australia and Tasmania, and it wouldn't be surprising if there were still some species that hadn't been discovered and identified.

Apparently there are some migratory species that fly over from the mainland and nest here for the summer. There might be species that only live in areas so remote that they have never been identified by science, let alone documented. There are species with only small populations, ones that ornithologists have simply never come across.

To interrupt his flow of consciousness for a moment, I mention the keas of New Zealand. At that he becomes even more excited and explains that research has shown that many species of parrot can reach the cognitive level of a five-year-old.

Sounds like a bit of an exaggeration to me. Lots of five-year-olds can read. Or at least operate the video recorder. Birds are primitive animals, only slightly more evolved than reptiles.

I say that any researcher that comes to that conclusion must have pretty interesting children themselves.

The guy doesn't get the joke.

We haul our rucksacks on to our backs. He says he hopes we have a nice day, as if we were going off for a picnic. Doughnut Boy hasn't got the faintest idea where we're headed. He can't put things in any order of importance.

'Kea: The Open-Programme Bird'
by Jiselle Ruby and Anthony Verloc

Over the last few decades the kea has demonstrated a clear determination to move closer to human settlements. This is down in part to an attempt to find sustenance but is also linked to these birds' need to explore and affect their surrounding environment.

In the national park at Arthur's Pass, keas destroyed a total of fourteen tents during a single summer season. At the car park in the same area of the park, the fabric roof of a jeep was torn to pieces, the upholstery on the seats was ripped open and all the wires within the dashboard were pulled apart in the space of only five days. In addition, windscreen wipers, the seals around windows, antennae and even tyres are all at risk. Some cases have been recorded in which the kea has succeeded in deflating the tyres by correctly opening the valves. With the help of its beak and talons it can easily manipulate objects and devices that normally demand human dexterity.

Some theorists consider this behaviour an example of social facilitation, which teaches younger individuals constantly to acquire new skills and to adapt their behaviour to an ever-changing environment.

SOUTH COAST TRACK, TASMANIA
Melaleuca to Farrell Point
Sunday, March 2007

HEIDI

It's sunny, and there's a gentle breeze, dry as tinder.

We've left the sludgy, boggy land and reached a plain slightly higher up. Dotted with clumps of grass, scrub and stunted bushes, the brown-green terrain is an undulating, rocky moorland – with no shade in sight. It's only now that I remember the suncream, and we stop to put some on. The path beneath our feet reveals how thin the layer of humus really is. Our hiking boots have scuffed it and broken it, like a layer of dry epidermis, making it crack and reveal the rough chalk-white gravel beneath. The path is like a thin, white ribbon stretching out in front of us, winding its way across the low-lying hills before veering off to the west.

The start of Old Port Davey Track feels good under foot – wonderful, rolling terrain. Melaleuca disappears behind us in less than an hour. The path roughly follows the Melaleuca lagoon inlet, which is nothing but a narrow sound that looks more like a river. Every now and then we catch a glimpse of the waters between the hills to our right.

There is nobody out here. Not a soul.

Although Southy felt wild and untamed, you could always sense the presence of other people. You knew you would meet other hikers at the campsites or see people overtaking you or walking in the opposite direction.

There were duckboards and fallen tree trunks made into bridges.

From the sheer scrawniness of this path, you can tell that walkers here are few and far between. In places it's almost entirely overgrown as it presses its way through the dense thicket. As you step on the path, rough twigs and small sharp leaves scratch at your calves. You can't see your feet; you think about snakes. Whenever we come across a slightly damper dip in the path, there is no trace of the muddy, boggy areas extended metres in both directions as trekkers prefer to walk around them, thus trampling the tussocks to a mush in ever increasing circles, a phenomenon we had seen back at Southy. Here you can see that the last time someone walked along here must have been last week some time. Or maybe last month. Or last year.

'Does anyone ever come out here?' I ask as, for the thousandth time, I'm yanking my hiking pole out of a thorny heather-like bush that has stretched its limbs across the path.

'This path isn't all that dramatic. It hasn't got features like Ironbound. And maybe this is too far away, too cut off. The guidebook only mentions this track in passing. Good job the map gives us timed legs for each day.'

'Only *in passing*?'

'Yes, it doesn't really go into much detail.'

Jyrki doesn't seem to understand that there's always a reason why particular treks become popular. The mere fact that a path exists is not the reason.

We continue like ants through a terrain that makes me feel smaller than at any other point until now.

This is like something straight out of Conrad.

The sun was low; and, leaning forward side by side, they seemed to be tugging painfully uphill their two ridiculous shadows of unequal length that trailed behind them slowly over the tall grass without bending a single blade.

JYRKI

Joan Point is noble.

The raised isthmus reaches out into Bathurst Channel like an outstretched finger: Go north, young man.

The treetops edge the beaches and the coves with a greenish foam. Other than that, the terrain is open. Resilient plants cover the hills like a coarse, grey-green layer of roughcast. Across the sound you can see Farrell Point low on the horizon and Lindsay Hill rising up behind it. Nothing but desolation as far as the eye can see. We're so high above sea level before descending towards the beach that, even from this distance, I can make out the next night's campsite. It's situated on the western side of Farrell, and there are trees there. Shade, protection from the wind.

I'd like to have seen this place when it was still covered with impenetrable pine forests. But it's still beautiful. It's not hard to see why this whole region is a World Heritage Site.

We're here together.

Just the two of us – and Tasmania.

Crossing Bathurst Narrows gives me the tingling sensation of traversing a strange final frontier. Like crossing the deathly quiet Styx, basking in the glowing afternoon light.

HEIDI

Bathurst Harbour is an enormous bay, a basin the size of a huge lake only separated from the sea by a narrow sound. It's partially sheltered by its steep shores and features a number of gentle, even peninsulas reaching out into the water.

I've never seen a place that would suit a hotel or a chalet complex better. That hillside over there is positively crying out to be terraced and fitted with rows of tidy holiday bungalows. Tourists could take boat trips to those islands over there. Cruise ships would chug out here all the way from Cockle Creek and lower their anchors at Bathurst Harbour Marina. Fair enough, there aren't any sandy beaches around here, but small yachts could quickly drive out towards the sea where there are dozens of small pristine golden beaches just waiting to welcome sun-worshippers. Mainland Australians would flood out here to cool off and breathe the purest air in the world; the innumerable secluded coves would provide prime locations for luxury villas.

There would be a road running along the even, eastern shore of Melaleuca Inlet, a road along which four-wheel-drive vehicles would shuttle holiday-makers to the serene shores of Fulton Cove.

It goes without saying that I'd get commission for all of this.

JYRKI

It can't be more than four o'clock by the time we've got the tent up, the beds made, collected water and gone for a wash.

Imagine what we could have achieved today if we'd carried on from Melaleuca and arrived here yesterday. This timetable has deteriorated so much that there's absolutely nothing to write home about any more.

Even crossing Bathurst, exciting as it was, didn't take up that much time, didn't make you feel like you'd done a decent day's leg. Although the journey was far longer than at New River Lagoon and the wind was strong enough that it kept pushing the dinghy to one side, the shenanigans with the boat were just more of the same. It's not an adventure any more; it's just an inconvenience.

The sky is almost entirely cloud-free. Only around the tops of the eucalyptus trees can we see a few fan-like cirrus clouds. It doesn't look like rain, but now that we've got plenty of time it's a good opportunity to have a rain drill.

I show her how to build a base on the ground in the vestibule using loose branches piled on top of each other, small palettes on which to place the rucksacks. You should always build these palettes every time you set up camp, no matter what the weather looks like. Just to be on the safe side. Everything you don't need inside the tent at night should be placed in watertight containers and packed into the rucksacks. Then you stretch the rain covers over the top. The rucksacks are placed inside the vestibule on top of the palettes. Then it can piss it down as much as it likes.

I reject a few of her attempts. The branches she's collected are twisted or too thin. Seeing as we've got so much time, we might as well learn things properly.

HEIDI

Finally we get the rucksacks standing in the vestibule like soldiers on parade, and I realize I'm absolutely starving. Yesterday's meal must have stretched my stomach, made it think similar quantities of grub would be on offer in the future, too.

Jyrki's sets up the cooker to boil some water; it looks like it's a mashed-potato day. I dig out the bag of food and take out the plastic bag of flatbread, Mountain Bread, as these tortilla-shaped pancakes are called. I look at the slices of bread through their plastic covering, and at first I think I'm seeing things.

Then I take a closer look. Oh *shit*.

I open up the bag. No, I haven't been seeing things.

The surface of the bread is covered with small, dark patches radiating out in lighter, greenish-grey blotches.

Mould.

I turn the packet in my hands. How am I going to tell him this, when there's still the matter of the missing pepperoni?

Thank God we had a decent meal yesterday; the taste of garlic still lingers in my mouth. How amazing it felt to fill my mouth with heaped spoonfuls of soft, juicy, slightly overcooked pasta. None of your *al dente* nonsense, but wonderful, pink-and-orange tomatoey baby food that you hardly needed to chew.

Jyrki looks over at me and the packet of bread. From the position of his eyebrows, you can tell he's sensed there's something wrong.

It's too late to back-pedal.

JYRKI

Half a packet of pepperoni – lost?

Three whole flatbreads – mouldy?

She asks whether we could cut off the good bits and eat them. I shake my head: the whole packet could be full of mould spores, and that means myco-toxins.

She asks whether we should just throw it away. I ask her where exactly she thinks she can throw something out here.

Then I enquire about what the hell happened to the slices of pepperoni.

She can't answer. They just disappeared into thin air.

I can feel my jaws tensing.

She sits down on the ground, props her arms on her knees and hides her face in her hands.

I hear her saying that she can go without something.

I give an unintentional sigh.

I quickly count things up in my head. Why did we have to go and eat rice cakes for breakfast 'for a change'? We should have eaten the things that were likely to go off first. There are still a few days before the bread's best-before date, but the bag was already opened – of course – and then came the dampest of damp nights at Cox Bight.

Without all this fuss they would have survived almost until the end of the trek. We've already eaten four rice cakes; only eight left. One each every morning.

We'll have rice cake with onion and tomato purée in the morning, I tell her. There's half an onion left. That's decent food, too. And as for the tomato purée – it's full of lycopene, which helps protect the skin from burning in the sun.

HEIDI

'I could carry the food from here on.'

There isn't all that much left, but I suppose he doesn't want to take the risk of anything else going missing.

The thought of his insinuations makes a red curtain descend before my eyes, and I can't stop myself.

'That's manly of you. Very chivalrous.'

It hits the spot.

Jyrki glowers at me, expressionless, so expressionless that I have to continue as if nothing had happened.

'What about me? Should I take the gas or the cooker?'

'How about you keep on carrying the rubbish?'

That mouldy bread? In my rucksack? No way.

The mere thought of that green rash on its surface growing and spreading, becoming furrier, sprouting disgusting light-grey hairs, and doing all this on my back, only a plastic film and a sliver of rucksack material away from my bare skin is enough to make me itch and shudder.

Once Jyrki is done with his tom yum tuna noodles and walks off into the woods with his little spade — out here in the oh so authentic wilderness there isn't even a pit toilet — I hand him the first few pages of Natural History Digest and start to think.

Those slices of bread will go mouldy, rot and biodegrade, for crying out loud. With the grateful help of all those mould spores, they have already begun their journey back into nature's grand recycling scheme.

Not in the bushes we've used as a toilet. Jyrki would see them straight away if he went to the loo again.

If I take them out of the plastic bag and leave them somewhere, the first rainfall will turn them to porridge and then all the lucky Tasmanian worms and happy little insects will take care of the rest.

I find a good spot a few metres behind the tent. There's a suitable hollow in among the tree roots, hidden by bushes at the front. I scrape up some loose leaves to cover them.

JYRKI

That night there's a great commotion going on behind the tent.

An animal or a group of animals has found something to eat. Maybe a bird of prey has found a small rodent. The sounds are like something out of the jungle. Scratching, flapping, scraping and scurrying.

She's sleeping as though nothing could possibly disturb her, breathing almost too evenly.

HEIDI

With any luck, here in the green dimness of the tent, comfortably tucked inside his sleeping-bag, his aching legs finally in a resting position, it'll be too much trouble to get up and see what's going on. I can hear Jyrki put down his guidebook for a moment, then hold it up again and bring it into the headlamp light.

Now that we're wrapped up inside, the thought of leaving the tent's safe womb is almost impossible; outside the Tasmanian night is alive and holding its own clandestine feast to which we have not been invited. I don't know whether I'd want to take part even if we had been invited.

Conrad forces his way into my mind, just as the fatigue is about to lull me to sleep.

And for a moment it seemed to me as if I also were buried in a vast grave full of unspeakable secrets. I felt an intolerable weight oppressing my breast, the smell of the damp earth, the unseen presence of victorious corruption, the darkness of an impenetrable night . . .

And just then Jyrki snaps, as an exceptionally loud thud can be heard from the bush. No, even closer than that. Through the chink in my eyelids I see him furrow his brow, put down his book, get up and unzip the tent door.

Feels warm next to my heart. There in my jacket pocket, glowing with its own heat. It's a butterfly, a claw, grown on to my chest, but still separate. At any moment I can take it out, and when it hits something stupid and annoying and irritating everything changes colour and the air turns and everything changes. Someone walking past, full of himself, he doesn't know how close it is. Guys shoving me about at the bus stop, talking shit, they don't know how close it is.

I can pull it out any time. You there, laughing, staring too much, the wrong look on your face. It will appear, ready to take a breath. It hisses as it draws air, then it's time. Any time. Any time it feels like it.

JYRKI

She's walking behind me, her head lowered.

I should have made her bury the rest of the bread properly, but there was almost nothing left of it.

When we stop to eat our muesli bars I show her the list of additives listed on the wrapper. I try to bring a note of reconciliation to my voice as I run my finger down the list and read the names out loud.

Everything that doesn't form part of wild animals' natural diet is potentially harmful. Refined sugar. Processed wheat. Hard fats. Salt — particularly salt.

She nods her head, but there's a stubborn look on her face.

That expression annoys me just enough that I feel I've got to put things a bit more pointedly. We have a responsibility to take care of our environment. Of course, any animal will eat something that tastes good and that it instinctively senses will give it sustenance. But animals can end up being poisoned. Animals can become ill just from the quantity of salt in some foods. Animals can react in unexpected ways to different food additives. Animals can develop behavioural anomalies.

I tell her about seagulls, crows and rats. No animal in this world is as unpleasant as one forcing its way outside its natural environment, feeding itself off human waste like a parasite. A creature eating only rubbish saturated in additives with no nutritional value will change its form and forget all about its evolution and its ecological niche.

I tell her about crow fledgelings whose mother feeds them with food she picks up at the bins outside fast-food restaurants. Because of this, the feathers in their wings grow so weak that the young birds will never be able to fly.

She gobbles down her muesli bar quickly, as easily as drawing breath, and I don't know whether she's listened to a word I've said.

HEIDI

'That's just the kind of thought process that's probably been left over from your job,' Jyrki lectures me, his nostrils as wide with indignation as if I'd just suggested his trekking equipment included a wooden cup and a flannel shirt. 'We feed people shit that's made to smell nice, and we don't give a damn about the lasting effects it might have. Just so long as they swallow it.'

The shock makes my teeth miss the final raisin in my muesli bar. Jyrki has never said a word about my work. At least he's never said anything to make me believe he has something against my job. Well, my former job, that is, but he doesn't know about that yet. He thinks I'm only on unpaid leave.

'Isn't it nice that at least one of us does something decent for a living. I mean, you sell poison — openly and with society's blessing.' I manage to find a lingering, unhurried tone in my voice. 'Shall we count up the bodies?'

Jyrki is taken aback; he wasn't expecting a counterattack. For a moment he has to fumble to find the right words.

'People know what they're doing. They know the risks. I can't be held responsible if customers walk into a pub completely compos mentis. I don't pour booze down their throats. You, on the other hand, create nets, then you ruthlessly drive people into them. You manipulate people and have them believe only spin, only see one side of things.'

By now my throat is totally dry.

'OK, we put ideas in people's heads. They either believe them or they don't. Your business makes its money by treating people like ducks in the park. You feed them for a while, then they can't live without you.'

Jyrki is silent like someone cut to the very core.

'And besides . . .' I can't help myself. The words just bubble from my muesli-sticky mouth. 'Besides, I don't work there any more. I quit. For this trip. I actually quit. So think about that: what have you really been prepared to sacrifice for all this? For anyone? I sacrificed my career.'

Jyrki stands up, his mouth set tightly and starts hauling his rucksack on to his back.

'And my hair.'

He doesn't respond, just slips his other arm through the strap and strides off in great bounding steps along the path, his lopsided hiking poles making him look endearingly crippled and imperfect.

JYRKI

We cross the shoulder of Lindsay Hill in utter silence. Yet again today's leg is for fucking lightweights. It's not easy; it's just far too short. For a while we walk at a higher altitude, about a hundred metres or so up. The path roughly follows Spring River, which looks like a frilly strip of verdant undergrowth to the left. The mouth of the river is in Page Bay, our last glimpse of the sea on this trip. A string of hills rises up on both sides of us: Erskine Range and Rugby Range. They are both about six hundred metres high, worn and curvaceous. By the early afternoon we've already started making our way down into the damp, almost boggy valley at Spring River.

Today might be a good opportunity to air the sleeping-bags properly, the silk bag liners, all our extra clothes. The tent floor could be cleaned of all the eider feathers that have come out of the bedding. Someone could scrape clean the rucksack pockets and seams of all the fine stubborn sand stuck in there. After all, there's plenty of time and idle hands.

HEIDI

I step into the bushes, crouch down, pour water over myself. The cool water is always a shock to the system as it runs along your warm back. It feels like acid. I soak off the layer of salt that has dried at the sides of my face and around my hairline. I splash my armpits, my neck, wipe away the grime and sand and sweat from around my calves, then look towards my crotch, where a weary-looking thread, reddened at the root, dangles limply between my legs.

I look at everything I have with me. My sarong, the wombat bottle, my clothes and a scrap of magazine – and the all-important resealable bag.

I reach down between my thighs, take a firm grip on the thread and pull. The tampon comes out gracefully, slippery with redness.

I stand upright and dangle it in my hand like a hunter examining a small rodent, perhaps weighing up its nutritional value. I look at it from all sides, this hazardous human waste, this podgy self-satisfied parasite that has sucked my blood and with whom I have an involuntary symbiotic relationship.

I straighten my body and raise my arm.

It starts spinning in a dizzying, deliberate circle, building up great centri-fugal force, so much so that I can almost feel the blood collecting at one end of the tampon.

And when I release my grip and let the tampon hurtle into the air, it flies, glides into the distance, so jubilantly that I can almost hear the air whistling. It reaches its zenith, then disappears in a glorious curve deep into the Tasmanian wilderness, and for a moment I am small yet defiant, the rebellious David, with his tiny, insignificant weapons, crushed on all sides by the mighty Goliath.

JYRKI

The moon shines brightly that night.

Our camp is protected by the trees, but if you look up you can see the stars.

For people used to the northern sky and the glow of city lights, seeing this sky is like diving into the depths of darkness. There are more stars than I've ever seen, as though sugar crystals had been sprinkled on black velvet, with the Milky Way running through the middle like a wide strip of silver dust. There are far more stars here than in the Northern Hemisphere, as the Southern Hemisphere faces right towards the centre of the Milky Way while the Northern only faces its edges.

Apart from the Southern Cross all the constellations are strange to me.

An alien sky.

This is the closest I'm going to get to being on another planet.

This is why I don't like staying in huts but want to sleep in the great outdoors.

She comes back from her evening piss. The LED light on her forehead kills the three-dimensional landscape in an instant. The brightness of the moon, filtered through the swaying boughs of the trees, is flattened into a wedge of banal light, into a two-dimensional photograph of a field of vision in which there are no longer any colours, any depth or subtlety.

Lanterns, the assassins of moonlight.

She goes into the tent. Once the LED light is only shining through the green fabric of the tent the magic returns, and the trees are bathed once again in glints of silver.

There's a sudden rustle in the bushes, so loud that it can't possibly be the wind.

Her startled voice comes out of the tent, asking what it was.

Maybe some representative of the local fauna has turned up looking to see if there's another party, I tell her.

'That animal has a charmed life,' he said; 'but you can say this only of brutes in this country. No man — you apprehend me? — no man here bears a charmed life.'

— Joseph Conrad, *Heart of Darkness*

SOUTH COAST TRACK, TASMANIA
Spring River to Watershed Camp
Tuesday, March 2007

JYRKI

The region opening up in front of us today has possibly the greatest name I've ever heard.

Lost World Plateau.

When I wake up that morning my first thought is that Melaleuca and the Tasmania infested with surfer dudes and aeroplanes is behind us now. And that's where it will stay. Two day's trekking and the sound at Bathurst separate us from them. Now we're on our own.

It sounds so good that if I were a poet I'd try to make it rhyme.

This solitude, it gives me kicks; now we've crossed the River Styx.

I stretch my limbs in the freshly hatched morning. I pour water from the Platypus into the pot and open up the cooker. I screw it on top of the gas cylinder and start fumbling in the side pocket of my rucksack for the lighter.

I haven't worried about the lighter running out of gas. Even though it's only a stupid little one I got at a kiosk – trivial, orange, smooth – you could use it to light the stove almost until the end of time. The flint will produce a spark long after the gas inside has run out.

But the lighter isn't in the left-hand pocket of my rucksack.

The pocket is slightly open, and I've always made sure to close the zip properly. Always.

HEIDI

Jyrki's agitated voice takes me aback as I try to perform the intricate ritual of emptying the air mattress.

'What use would I have for it?'

'It's not in the pocket.'

I crawl obediently out of the tent to share in his confusion. 'It was you that last used it yesterday evening.'

'Yes, and I put it back where I've always put it.'

'Sure it didn't accidentally end up in the pot? Or in the food bag?'

Jyrki rummages in the woefully measly bag of food, then over-dramatically tips the entire contents out on to the mat of eucalyptus leaves.

'Is it here? Is it?'

I have to admit that it is not.

'What the fuck are we going to do now? All our food needs to be cooked.'

Well, that's not strictly true, as we've still got a couple of rice cakes, but . . .

Right then I remember something and dart back inside the tent, take out my bumbag and dig around for a minute. The matches from the bar in Spain. I find the packet, and behind the card with the scratch strip at the back there are still four cardboard saviours. I hold the matches out of the tent door.

'Here. I've got a light.'

Jyrki looks at me, and for a moment it seems as though he could light a fire with his eyes.

'Four?'

'Better than nothing, isn't it?'

'We've still got days to go. Cooking dinner alone will use them.'

'Are you sure you've looked everywhere?'

Yes, he is.

JYRKI

We skip boiling water for morning tea. Instead, we wash down our rice cakes with water shaken together with a little sugar. We're almost out of the sugar we took from the aeroplane, too. Neither of us normally uses sugar in tea or coffee. Out here we add some for its carbohydrate value.

Cardboard matches and scratch strips. They could let you down at any moment, won't light anything, flare up and go out straight away. They could be blown out by a sudden gust of wind.

I can feel the nervousness in my stomach. I can somehow understand the pepperoni. She's probably eaten it. It would be obscenely disloyal but just about understandable. I can even understand her record-breaking stupidity with the bread. But why steal the lighter and hide it? Revenge? For *what*?

When she says there was a shelf full of matches at the hut in Melaleuca I'm a blood-red millisecond away from slapping her.

In retaliation I point out that if we'd stuck to my original timetable we'd have arrived in Scott's Peak today and be putting our feet up in the comfort of the bus by midday.

I look at them from above, high up. Them and their tiny little world, each one of them running about, important, busy hurrying here and there. Then I push my stick into the nest and stir.

SOUTH COAST TRACK, TASMANIA
Spring River to Watershed Camp
Tuesday, March 2007

HEIDI

The path has risen up, twisting its way through hills covered in shrubs and bushes, and our journey is now clearly taking us further inland. Behind us, somewhere along the coast, was once Port Davey, now nothing but dust. People must have used this path to reach it since time immemorial.

The inclines along this path aren't particularly steep, but there's no shade in sight. Now that the rush of the sea is far behind us, I feel the full effect of the ear-splitting silence. I can sense fear lurking in the silence.

The proximity of the sea represents security. If I got lost in Tasmania — which would be the easiest thing in the world in all these undulating plains, dotted all the way to the horizon with identical bushes and scrub spewed up from the ground that remind me of those clusters of trees you see on the savannahs of Africa — I'd feel an immediate sense of relief upon hearing the roar of the waves, even if I were still in the middle of nowhere. The sea is always a thoroughfare, even if you don't have a boat. The sea is water, even though you can't drink it. At sea your eyes can gaze out into the distance, unhindered.

Here there's no security.

Here the air seems obscured by a dim haze.

I push my sunglasses, which have slid down to the end of my nose, back into place. It occurs to me that I must have performed that same action hundreds of times in the last few days. What's going on? These glasses fitted perfectly a couple of weeks ago.

'Can a person's head shrink?'

Jyrki turns his head and looks at me slowly. I can see myself reflected in his Serengetis as two small convex insects.

'Your head? Shrink?'

'Yes. Look at this.'

I clench the muscles in my face and again my glasses slip obediently down to the end of my nose.

'Wipe away the sweat and suncream underneath.'

'They didn't seem to mind the sweat and suncream in New Zealand. Tasmania has shrunk my head.'

Jyrki stares at me.

'I see. Well, I suppose your face could have become a bit thinner in that time.'

It must be true. I haven't looked in the mirror for over a week. Because I've been wearing the same clothes all the time, I haven't noticed any changes. If they've felt a bit loose, I've just put it down to them stretching from not being washed.

I look down. My thighs stick out of my shorts like a pair of lean snakes.

JYRKI

For her, Tasmania is an enormous magical creature that treats us whatever way it wants. She probably imagines we're like two dogged inquisitive ants trekking across Tasmania's belly. We trip over its body hair, get stuck in its pores and try not to disturb its sleep. And because we're walking along Tasmania's thin, sensitive skin, there's always the possibility that at some moment, after some tossing and turning, the creature will wake up once and for all. Then a hand will appear above us, so huge and fast that we won't even register it until just before it violently descends with a crashing, crushing thump.

HEIDI

I don't know whether it's a fact or whether I'm just imagining it, but today's leg seems incredibly long compared with the previous couple of days, and my head feels giddy and woozy.

But it would be stupid to start complaining.

A solemn truce seems to have been established between us.

For some reason I start thinking about an apple.

It would be round and entertainingly smooth, so symmetrical it could almost have been made by human hands. It would be a Granny Smith or an Antonovka: greenish, sour and with crisp skin. As my teeth sink into it a chunk of apple would snap into my mouth, oozing sweet, acrid juices across my tongue and gums.

The succulent fruit would crunch between my teeth. I would eat right up to the core. I would gnaw every piece of flesh from around the pips, all the bits I wouldn't normally eat. I might even eat the core, too, and enjoy the strong nutty flavour of the pips.

For the first half of the day the path winds its way through the hilly open country — I've seen plenty of hills before, thanks very much — then we start our descent into wetlands where the path is overgrown.

And I mean really overgrown.

The knee-high scrub that smothered the path leading away from Melaleuca was one thing, but this is thick thorny bush reaching high above us and poking our ribs on both sides. Branches and twigs twine together in front of us, and all the while there is a terrific rattling and rustling as Jyrki attempts to clear the path using only his body mass. Branches freed from one another flick backwards and hit me in the face as soon as he has passed them.

In places it's hard to make out the path at all, you've just got to step in approximately the right direction and assume that your foot will find some flattish ground beneath the foliage.

The dips in the path are filled with mud — sometimes they're pretty deep, too — and for the first time since crossing Red Point Hills Jyrki's impaired hiking pole causes us real problems: it sinks deep into the ground without any warning, and because it's hollow it's always getting stuck.

This goes on and on and on. And on.

Out here you need a machete. Seriously.

I think about the leeches and shiver. Brainless creatures, but bloodthirsty ones. Lurking in the bushes. Fat and blood-sucking. But they normally only come out after rainfall, and the weather has been bone dry ever since the downpour at Cox Bight.

Leeches.

What would Mr Conrad say?

But the wilderness had found him out early, and had taken on him a terrible vengeance for the fantastic invasion.

JYRKI

I see something on the path.

At first I don't even realize what it is, it's so strange and out of place. But when I identify it my brain starts to boil with rage.

How can someone be so offensive, so indifferent, so . . . I can't even find words to describe someone that would do a thing like this.

Right there in the middle of the path is a used tampon. A cloud of flies is having a banquet on it.

Not only has someone had the nerve to throw something like that on the ground, they had to leave it right in the middle of the path, almost in protest. I'm surprised they didn't have a shit next to it for good measure.

After everything that's happened I suspect the culprit is very close indeed. It would make sense, but it's also an impossibility. We're already a good day's trek from yesterday's campsite.

It also annoys me that someone else has walked along this path so recently. I assumed we would be very, very alone.

I assumed a woman hiker would be something of a rarity out here.

I assumed what we had achieved was something profound.

The refuse is fresh. We're only about an hour's hike from the boggy riverbanks at Watershed and the designated campsite waiting for us. There must be other people there now.

I'm so repulsed that I can't even bring myself to say anything. I kick this desecration of the landscape into the bushes with a quick jolt of the foot, and the flies shoot upwards like a sheet of black upside-down rain.

I ask if the oil rag will burn for sure. Ante's there; can't see Kenu. The new guy's called Liquorice Fish.

The Fish says he's done it with crumpled bits of paper with candle wax inside. People don't get post through the door these days, so there's nothing to catch fire. Before you'd have had the newspaper and other bits of paper, letters and shit like that. Nowadays you're lucky if there's a fucking doormat. If your luck's out, it'll be just a tiled floor. That'll never ever light.

I'm like, it won't light, man, 'cos I've just pissed through that letterbox. I get through dozens of them in a day, and the Fish cracks up.

He says there's sometimes only a stupid gap between the two doors so, no matter how well you've got things started, the space is so small that only people's shoes'll burn before the fire runs out of oxygen and starts pouring smoke out into the stairwell.

Fuck stairwells and oxygen, says Ante. You seriously telling me you think about this shit?

Ante's foot is twitching, although he's not on nothing — not even coffee. His foot's tapping the floor, dododododoom.

Ante doesn't know what to do with himself if he's got to sit still. His life disappears if he hasn't got any action going down.

I ask about those outdoor letterboxes, what about them, but the Fish says they're for fucking amateurs.

HEIDI

I awake to the pangs of an empty stomach.

I think I must have been dreaming about smoked ham. Its smell is sensual, intoxicating; I can feel it in my mouth and my nostrils. I open my mouth and try to take a bite. I want to feel the pink succulence all the way up to my gums; I want the slab of meat to be thick as a fist, complete with a strip of white shining fat.

My eyes snap open, and in the dark-green dim of the tent I realize – because I can just make out my hand moving towards my mouth – that it's almost morning.

We're at Watershed.

This is by far the most dismal of all the 'campsites' I've seen in Tasmania. This is nothing but a patch of damp mossy scrub. It was almost impossible to find a spot of ground flat enough to put up the tent among the fallen trees and the brush. We could easily have thought we were in the wrong place, but our position on the map by the shallow river and the timing of our arrival meant there was no doubt about it.

The aroma of smoked ham is still hanging in the air.

'Jyrki?'

Jyrki rolls over in annoyance and mutters something indistinct. My overly tense tone of voice eventually has him wide awake.

'Does it smell of smoke round here, or is it just me?'

Jyrki sits up in his sleeping-bag. His once so magnificent shaved head, now sprouting only the pitiable grey down of a condor fledgeling, nudges the top of the tent, although he's not even fully upright. His nostrils widen, and again I find myself thinking of the kea in Kepler.

Jyrki sniffs the air.

'But it's just been raining. Pissed it down.'

'But that was on Friday.'

'Yeah, and it was coming down in buckets.'

I listen to my heart pounding, its tiny little legs beating nervously and frantically against the floor of its non-existent room.

Conrad whispers in my ear.

We could not understand because we were too far and could not remember because we were travelling in the night of first ages, of those ages that are gone, leaving hardly a sign — and no memories.

JYRKI

The air's maybe a bit hazy, but I don't really agree about the smell.

It could have been an illegal bonfire, but still — there's nobody else around here. Watershed is hardly what you'd call an open-plan campsite, but although we might not have seen anyone it would still have been impossible not to hear other voices. In that case I'd have had a word with them about how to dispose of certain personal-hygiene items.

After putting my Crocs on and going for a slash, a dark-red mist flashes momentarily in front of my eyes as I glance down at my hiking boots standing in the vestibule.

So that's her idea of humour.

The blue-black laces of one boot are neatly criss-crossed between the hooks, making it look like a daintily corseted waist. Compared with the other one, that is, which is missing something without which it is nothing: its bootlace.

The boot's tongue droops, obscene and impotent.

Hang on a minute.

Nelson Lakes.

Speargrass Hut.

The hustle and bustle that filled the porch that morning when some of the rucksacks had been torn open and the bootlaces, keys and insoles had disappeared.

What was it the ornithologist said back at Melaleuca? And the ranger at Kepler?

'Kea: The Open-Programme Bird'
by Jiselle Ruby and Anthony Verloc

For decades New Zealand farmers have considered the kea a pest that harms sheep. This notion has been widely criticized, as, particularly during the winter, flocks of sheep often graze unsupervised for months. During this time individual sheep can be lost for a number of different reasons.

Naturally, from the farmers' point of view, it is important to establish whether the kea feeds on the bodies of sheep that have died of illness or in an accident or whether the kea, in fact, precipitates the sheep's death. One would think that a relatively small bird would have difficulty killing an animal many times its size. However, there have been numerous reliable accounts of keas landing on a sheep's back, using their talons to grab hold of its wool, then systematically beating a wound into the sheep's skin with their beaks. These wounds are generally found in the area around the kidneys, where such a wound will in all probability cause massive trauma.

Examination of wounds of differing degrees of severity has demonstrated that the kea first tries to make a small incision in the sheep's skin, then inserts its curved beak and uses a rocking motion to further hollow the wound out. Some sheep have been found with holes the size of a fist in their skin. In some instances the kea has passed as far as the sheep's stomach cavity. More extreme theories have suggested that, in these cases, the kea can then pull out the sheep's internal organs until the animal eventually dies.

It is clear that such a substantial wound can lead to death, particularly in young or weak sheep. Recent research has, however, indicated that the kea's actions may be considerably more complex than previously thought. Namely, sheep attacked by the kea do not normally die of the injuries sustained in the attack but of blood poisoning caused by the *Clostridium* bacteria living in the earth. According to one theory, the kea deliberately transfers *Clostridium* spores into the wounds via trace elements of soil in its beak. The increase in *Clostridium* infections has led some farmers to vaccinate their flocks against blood poisoning. There has also been a number of discoveries of carcasses which display wounds inflicted by the kea but which have been only partially consumed.

In terms of evolution, the kea's carnivorous behaviour can be seen to stem from the time when moa birds dominated New Zealand's fauna. At this time the moa competed with the kea for vegetation, although moa carcasses provided the kea with an additional source of nourishment. Once the Maoris had hunted the moa into extinction, a gap appeared in the kea's protein-rich diet. This gap was only filled with the arrival of European settlers and their sheep. As masters of adaptability, in the intervening years the kea returned to its staple diet of vegetation, nuts, insects and slugs.

In any case, it seems clear that the arrival of the Europeans and their sheep provided the kea with a new, plentiful food source, the extensive use of which attests to a certain parallel between keas and humans: when there is plenty of food and obtaining it is relatively simple, the very act of hunting can become a pastime in its own right

HEIDI

Jyrki is explaining his parrot theory, and in a flash I realize that it applies not only to the lighter and the bootlace – the only items he brings up – but to my wombat bottle and the pepperoni, too, and a wave of embarrassment washes over me. I should have realized. Ages ago.

On top of that, I feel a very strong and real sense of guilt now that he no longer suspects me of everything. I haven't done any of those things, but I know that I *could* have done them, that I might even have *wanted* to do them, and it's written all over my face.

And, after all, I did do one thing.

'This boot was hardly made for walking.'

'Let's use one of the guy-lines. Get the penknife, cut off a bit long enough. I'm sure we can make do with twenty centimetres less of the stuff. We'll get more of it somewhere.'

Jyrki shakes his head.

'You know how much this tent cost?'

'Haven't you got any emergency spares?'

Jyrki's expression almost floors me.

'Yeah, they're with the spare pot, the spare sleeping-bag and the spare tent.'

That's right. Weight-hysterics again. All Jyrki's equipment is fundamentally indestructible and impossible to lose. Even his bootlaces are nylon-strengthened Cabelas, and because the pair of laces was relatively new a spare pair would have been nothing but pointless dead weight to carry around.

Just then Jyrki's face almost lights up as he remembers something, and he takes his hiking pole and starts pulling the duct tape from around the side. His expression freezes when he sees how little of it is left.

I've taped along the seam of my trousers, both inside and out, so that it'll hold together, and way past the end of the tear, too, just in case, and some of the tape might have been wasted.

Jyrki doesn't say anything but stares at the span of tape in his fingers.

'Hey. The gauze. We've got plenty of it left, and if you twist it tightly enough, it'll be strong as twine. That should hold it for a while . . .'

Jyrki doesn't go for it, presumably because it's my idea. Instead he limps onwards like a martyr in his unlaced boot.

'This'll have to do.'

We look at one another, our rucksacks packed and propped by our feet, a single rice cake in our stomachs. Another eight-hour leg ahead of us. I attempt a faint smile. It's not the end of the world – except, it is. I'm so exhausted that I'd like to collapse right here. I want to melt, let my bones and muscles dissolve into the Tasmanian earth and sink beneath the cracked dry surface into the heaving black muds below. It would be quiet there. It would be dark.

Jyrki looks at me expectantly, impatiently.

Conrad whispers in my ear again.

The wilderness had taken him, loved him, embraced him, got into his veins, consumed his flesh, and sealed his soul to its own by the inconceivable ceremonies of some devilish initiation.

I haul the rucksack on to my back. I can't understand how it's suddenly become so heavy, seeing as we seem to have been losing everything and using things up. At the spots where the frame touches my body, it feels at once sore and rough, as though my skin were hard and callused yet still grazed raw. It's neither of these things. I've checked.

Of course. We have to cross the deep, rocky section of Watershed Brook along a thin fallen tree trunk covered in slippery lichen.

I've got knots in my stomach, and my head is spinning as I stagger along the trunk, first tiptoeing then lurching forwards and almost falling against the branch providing something to hold on to.

I almost hope I fall into the brook. I do hope I fall into the brook. I hope I sprain my ankle and have to lie down for two days. I hope, while I'm lying there, that a line of little roast potatoes marches into my mouth.

Just as I get to the other side I hear a sound.

It's far away, but it's getting closer all the time. At first I think it's an insect buzzing frantically near by, but the sound is regular and seems to be getting louder too steadily.

Before long the drone is ear-splitting.

A helicopter.

Its sound is oppressively loud, and the upper branches of the eucalyptus trees shimmer as it hovers close above us before speeding off once again up into the sky.

'They operate tourist flights around here, too, then,' Jyrki scoffs and dives from the banks of the brook into what appears to be a hillside covered with impenetrable scrub.

It's cloudy, strangely and miserably cloudy, and the sky is dim and grey.

There's a bum lying beside the wall. True to form, his mug's blue and ruddy, straggly stubble growing in patches, and his clothes are shitty. He's out like a light. The winter sun was presumably shining on that spot a while ago; he's decided to sit down, and now drink and exhaustion have finally got the better of him.

Liquorice Fish glances at the rest of us. He sticks his hand in his pocket, takes out a handful of coins and counts them.

That'll do, he says. One of yous, go the Shell station and fill a litre-and-a-half Coke bottle with petrol. If anyone asks, say Dad's testing his outboard motor.

Ante gives a nervy laugh, Ante-style. A giggle-chuckle.

I get the neck tingles again, hollower, itchier than ever. A hot-cold sensation washes from my stomach up to my head.

Who's going? asks Liquorice Fish. Yous two stay here and make sure he don't go anywhere before we've had our fun and games.

Anyone got a lighter?

I've got one, I pipe up and take it out of my pocket. Small and smooth and orange.

SOUTH COAST TRACK, TASMANIA
Watershed Camp to River Crossing
Wednesday, March 2007

JYRKI

Every now and then the sound of the helicopter fades into the distance, then comes closer again. At least the small aeroplanes going backwards and forwards to and from Melaleuca only went past once a day. The magnificent Bathurst lagoon and the landscape around here must be popular with flight tourists in Hobart, but that chopper's continual coming and going doesn't exactly put you in the mood for hiking.

It's like being in Switzerland. It was there that I once saw a flying cow. It must have been a piece of prime livestock, as they'd gone to the trouble of flying it around from A to B, attached to a long harness dangling beneath the belly of a helicopter, right there in the middle of all that relatively untouched Alpine scenery. I thanked my lucky stars Daisy didn't shit herself with fright just as they were flying overhead.

The path leads us deeper into a secluded tangle of little ditches and gullies. Annoyingly, the helicopter seems to be clacking constantly right above the covering of branches where we're walking. I'd love to get a look at the damned thing and give those gawping tourists the finger, but we always seem to be stuck in the middle of the thickest scrub in the world every time the chattering of the blades comes closer.

I point out that even if we were James Bond and his curvaceous sidekick, no matter how we tried there could be no better way of hiding from people looking for us from the air.

She doesn't even snigger.

I tell her about the flying cow, but even that doesn't trigger any reaction.

My left boot is flopping around. The broken pole is more trouble than it's worth going uphill. I've never been so infuriatingly slow. At last we reach the shoulder of the nameless hill next to Davey Sugarloaf.

All I can do is take a deep breath.

HEIDI

Gustave Doré. That's what I said to Bill back in the Grampians.

As we dive out of the bush and on to the ridge, Doré hits us right in the retina.

The sky is a sickening greyish-red.

I've never seen anything like it.

The sun, which we weren't able to see properly in the morning as it rose from the south-east, obscured from where we were camped, now looks like an angry, cinnabar brown eye; like a long-buried bronze coin in the middle of the swirling, heaving sky.

There's no longer any doubt about the smell of smoke; it hangs in the air, thick and bitter, and the whole horizon is shrouded in grey and black, more sinister and oppressive than any storm clouds, and along the lower edge of the cloud mass radiates a dirty orange glow.

My heart curls up like a dying insect.

Shit, says Jyrki, more to himself than to me.

He pulls the map out of his shorts pocket.

He starts bombarding me with short sharp observations like a stenographer stuck on high-speed. The wind is blowing from the north-west; between us and the fire there is a wide river, a billabong and a range of hills.

'Let's go back to Watershed,' I say as I recall the clammy dampness and shade of the campsite, the lichen and the deep, cool brook. With all its moss and mosquitoes the place seemed like God's very own sponge; you just couldn't set it on fire, not even if you doused it in petrol first.

Jyrki shakes his head.

I remember how much he hates retracing his own footsteps, but I don't say anything.

'Our best shot is to try and reach River Crossing,' he says. 'It's a proper river, and according to the map it's wide and deep. Watershed's only a brook. You really don't want to be back at Watershed when all those trees catch fire.'

I recall Bill's stories from the Grampians, and I swallow and nod, although every step towards the red-grey horizon makes me cough.

And now . . . What's that?

It's floating down from the sky. It's got a friend.

Thousands of friends.

It's raining light, white flakes of ash.

My legs, which only a few days ago were like bouncy springs, feel stiff and only move when I tell them to, as I stagger after Jyrki down towards the plateau.

JYRKI

It's raining, she says. She sounds relieved.

It's true; it is raining.

First came the ash. Now there's a very, very hesitant drizzle of water.

The isolated droplets are almost as heavy as hailstones. When they hit my rucksack, they leave little white stains. Ash-hearts.

Forest fires do this sometimes. So much heat rushes up into the atmosphere that moisture eventually collects around the particles of ash creating small, localized showers, a caricature of rain.

She might have been right in suggesting we go back to Watershed. But now that the fire's so close, I know the winds will push the blaze a damn sight faster uphill than downhill. And we're going downhill. Not much, but still.

I try to force my legs to move faster, but I'm like a cripple in these boots. Filling my lungs with air is starting to get a bit difficult.

HEIDI

It's almost dark, although it's only two o'clock. I've had to take my sunglasses off. The drizzling or, rather, the splashing of the rain didn't last long. Jyrki didn't seem to be especially happy about the rain, and he hasn't mentioned the fact that it's stopped.

I hurry along the path, out of breath, stiff, but so briskly that Jyrki is sometimes left behind until he, in an irritable imploring voice, points this out, and I realize what it must be like trekking without a bootlace. The boot must be nothing more than a burden, a hindrance, as though someone had tied a dead weight to his foot.

Thankfully the terrain is fairly flat for once, but in excruciatingly typical fashion the path to Old Port Davey Track is covered in thigh-height, overgrown scrub, and all the while I know with aching, exhausted clarity that we should stop and eat or drink something but that we can't because there's chaos and turmoil behind the hills, and the air is thick, so very thick, and I can't even suggest having a break although I'm starting to feel faint.

This is how humans function. This is precisely how humans function. You know what lies behind the horizon, but you have to carry on in the same direction because that's what you've been doing, that's what you've decided, and changing direction or turning back would be a sign of giving in, of letting go of everything you've achieved so far.

You keep going, fast, although you know only too well what lies ahead.

JYRKI

First I feel the wind.

The wind is so strong that it makes my shorts flap erratically, and it's hot as a dragon's breath.

I stop. I can see the fear in her eyes.

I hear a low growl.

Then a sound, followed by a thick ragged crack that can't be anything else but . . .

A eucalyptus tree bursting with the sheer profuseness of its sap.

I see the first flicker of flames from behind the hills.

She's already dropped her guard once before. How can I protect her from the roaring, blistering wall of flames rising up behind the horizon?

For the first time I realize how important she's become to me. That, and how and why I've brought her here, right into the heart of darkness.

HEIDI

Oh God, this is it.

The sound isn't dissimilar from that of the tide. It's surprisingly similar, in fact; growling, shoving the world out of its way, filling your eardrums with its terrifying roar. It's a beast that'll devour everything in its path.

It'll close the sky. Just like that. You'll see it happen right before your eyes. In a flash.

It'll close the earth.

It'll churn out a suffocating darkness and suck the oxygen from the air in heaving gulps.

It's a world that was begging to be set alight.

And at that moment I catch sight of something I should never have seen.

The horror! The horror!

From the ridge, a herd of wallabies dashes towards me, hysterical mothers with joeys in their pouches. I catch sight of their little ears as they flash past, and in the chaotic hurricane of life forms I see a wombat galloping clumsily onwards. The wombat, the animal I've never seen save for its charming poo and that I've always wanted to see in the wild – No! We weren't supposed to meet like this – it hurtles past me, almost toppling me, big and stocky, and with claws that could easily kill a large dog . . .

A thud. Another.

Birds are falling from the sky like enormous, dark hailstones.

Now I can see the flames.

All my limbs lose their ability to move. I stare up at the ridge as though a taut, painful thread were running from my eyes and holding my gaze fast.

Still holding the map, Jyrki tears the rucksack from my back, throws it to the ground, pushes me off the path and shouts, 'Run, run!' But bloody hell – *he's* still carrying his own rucksack. And my stiff log-legs stagger onwards, we're running, and I keep tripping over tussocks and brushwood, and somewhere behind us a dizzying, crackling wall is coming closer, so close that I can already feel the heat, and with every hysterical hiccupping breath I haul my lungs full of something hot and stinging and –

I feel a sharp shove in my back, my feet leave the ground and my mouth is suddenly full of mud. I'm lying in a tiny narrow brook so shallow that my stomach barely gets wet. I can just feel my clothes soaking up the pathetic dribble of water at the bottom of the brook when an eighty-kilo weight lands on my back. Eighty kilos and a rucksack, walloping the air from my lungs. Again the taste of mud; the Tasmanian spring water sluices against my chin and the sudden change in temperature makes my teeth wince.

'Jyrki.'

'Try and breath just above the surface of the water. Take a piece of cloth, soak it. The fumes'll be around us any minute.'

'Jyrki, get into the water!'

'Too shallow. The rucksack'll protect me.'

Jyrki presses me down towards the bottom of the brook; save for my back, my clothes are already heavy with the water, and Jyrki's arms refuse to do anything but force me further towards the protecting dampness.

'Jyrki, I'm –'

'Shh!'

Shh what? I think in spite of it all. Can't I say before we die that nobody else would ever have thrown themselves on top of me to protect me with the only body they'll ever own? And just then I hear what he must have heard above the roar, and a moment later the weight is lifted from my back, arbitrarily bruising the small of my back and the insides of my knees as it rises, and for half a second I raise my eyes from the mud.

Jyrki is standing behind me, a frantic silhouette, the wall of fire a couple of hundred metres off, coughing and waving his long, lanky arms in the air.

Now I too hear the rattling of the helicopter.

The helicopter.

The registration book.

We wrote down our names and our route back in Melaleuca.

I have to hold my head down, because the fumes are already so thick, and suddenly I feel a rush of air, someone hauling me upwards, and now I realize, finally, that this is it.

I can see flames and hear a hoarse shrieking, voices ringing with mortal fear and panic — and with good reason, because everything in sight is ablaze. My heart's pounding, almost bursting, because this is exactly what I wanted.

For a moment it feels as though I'm dreaming, just about to wake up, but I shake the thought from my mind because this is good.

And then I'm in the air; with a few beats of my wings I rise up higher and look down at the two of them staggering around, their heads bowed, caps covering their mouths as they stumble forwards, tripping over the scrub, their legs taut as they run, crouched low so that the blades whirring above don't take off their scalps.

The metallic bee shoots upwards, swaying, the flames almost singeing its iron legs.

There's fire all around. Hot, cleansing fire. Black, fertile soot.

A moment ago it was still in these claws, the colour of sunset, small and smooth — and, now, behold.

I swoop lazily, buoyed in a jet of hot air, and look down at the mark I've left on the world.

There was no sign on the face of nature of this amazing tale that was not so much told as suggested to me in desolate exclamations, completed by shrugs, in interrupted phrases, in hints ending in deep sighs.

— Joseph Conrad, *Heart of Darkness*

NOT BEFORE SUNDOWN
Johanna Sinisalo
978-0-7206-1350-6 • paperback • 240pp • £9.99

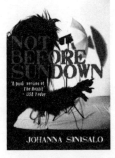

'A sharp, resonant, prickly book that exists on the slipstream of SF, fantasy, horror and gay fiction.' – Neil Gaiman

'Chillingly seductive' – *Independent*

'A punk version of *The Hobbit*' – *USA Today*

A young photographer, Mikael, finds a small, man-like creature in his courtyard: a troll, known from Scandinavian mythology as a demonic wild beast, a hybrid like the werewolf, and supposedly extinct. Mikael takes him home but soon discovers that trolls exude pheromones that smell like Calvin Klein aftershave and have a profound aphrodisiac effect on all those around him. But what Mikael and others who come into contact with the troll fail to learn, with tragic consequences, is that the troll is the interpreter of man's darkest, most forbidden desires.

A bestseller in Finland and translated into ten languages *Not Before Sundown* (*Troll: A Love Story* in the USA) is a multi-award-winning novel of sparkling originality and a wry, peculiar and beguiling story of nature and man's relationship with wild things and of the dark power of the wildness within us.

Peter Owen books can be purchased from:
Central Books, 99 Wallis Road, London E9 5LN, UK
Tel: +44 (0) 845 458 9911 Fax: + 44 (0) 845 458 9912
e-mail: orders@centralbooks.com

www.peterowen.com

NINA IN UTOPIA
Miranda Miller

978-0-7206-1355-1 • paperback • 240pp • £9.95

'A gifted and highly articulate novelist.'
– *Glasgow Herald*

Time travel, Bedlam and the mad Victorian painter Richard Dadd all feature in *Nina in Utopia*, the latest novel by Miranda Miller, one of the most original novelists working in Britain today.

Traumatized by the death of her little daughter in 1854, Nina, the wife of an ambitious doctor, finds herself in London a hundred and fifty years later. As a tourist in the twenty-first century, she believes she has found a Utopia where the grime, poverty and violence of Victorian London have been expunged. She befriends Jonathan, an architect and – shockingly for Nina's Victorian sensibilities – divorcee, who introduces her to the myriad wonders of modern life, including television, curry and clubbing. When she returns to her own time after a long weekend, her husband takes fright on hearing of her experiences and has her committed to Bedlam, where she is a contemporary of the fairy painter Richard Dadd. Here she finds another Utopia in the care of a doctor with modern ideas on patient rehabilitation. Yearning for that magical week-end, however, Jonathan and Nina reach out to one another across the centuries . . .

Peter Owen books can be purchased from:
Central Books, 99 Wallis Road, London E9 5LN, UK
Tel: +44 (0) 845 458 9911 Fax: + 44 (0) 845 458 9912
e-mail: orders@centralbooks.com

www.peterowen.com

Also published by Peter Owen

LOVING MEPHISTOPHELES
Miranda Miller

978-0-7206-1275-2 • paperback • 312pp • £11.95

'A wonderfully generous novel, several books wrapped into one, and I would have been very happy to stay with any of the strands or in any of the places it takes us to – I was particularly struck by the recreations of Edwardian London and of the London of the modern homeless. It's an epic narrative full of energy, with the wild and joyful inventiveness of an Angela Carter story. It is enjoyable and ingenious, and I hope it will find many readers.'
– Hilary Mantel

When Jenny, a third-rate music-hall chanteuse, remarks to her mentor and lover Leo, aka the Great Pantofsky, that she never wants to grow old, she doesn't know quite who she's speaking to. Her contract to love him will reside at the Metaphysical Bank in High Street Kensington – for ever.

As Leo gleefully exploits the rich offerings of twentieth-century London – as a magician, fighter pilot, coke dealer and City banker – Jenny finds that the joy of eternal youth is more ambiguous than one might think. With the strain of constantly having to reinvent herself as her own offspring and watching friends, lovers and family pass, she begins to regret her decision. But it is when she becomes pregnant with a daughter that Leo's true nature and that of her pact is revealed.

Peter Owen books can be purchased from:
Central Books, 99 Wallis Road, London E9 5LN, UK
Tel: +44 (0) 845 458 9911 Fax: + 44 (0) 845 458 9912
e-mail: orders@centralbooks.com

www.peterowen.com

SOME AUTHORS WE HAVE PUBLISHED

James Agee • Bella Akhmadulina • Tariq Ali • Kenneth Allsop
Alfred Andersch • Guillaume Apollinaire • Machado de Assis • Miguel Angel Asturias
Duke of Bedford • Oliver Bernard • Thomas Blackburn • Jane Bowles • Paul Bowles
Richard Bradford • Ilse, Countess von Bredow • Lenny Bruce • Finn Carling
Blaise Cendrars • Marc Chagall • Giorgio de Chirico • Uno Chiyo • Hugo Claus
Jean Cocteau • Albert Cohen • Colette • Ithell Colquhoun • Richard Corson
Benedetto Croce • Margaret Crosland • e.e. cummings • Stig Dalager • Salvador Dalí
Osamu Dazai • Anita Desai • Charles Dickens • Fabián Dobles • William Donaldson
Autran Dourado • Yuri Druzhnikov • Lawrence Durrell • Isabelle Eberhardt
Sergei Eisenstein • Shusaku Endo • Erté • Knut Faldbakken • Ida Fink
Wolfgang George Fischer • Nicholas Freeling • Philip Freund • Carlo Emilia Gadda
Rhea Galanaki • Salvador Garmendia • Michel Gauquelin • André Gide
Natalia Ginzburg • Jean Giono • Geoffrey Gorer • William Goyen • Julien Gracq
Sue Grafton • Robert Graves • Angela Green • Julien Green • George Grosz
Barbara Hardy • H.D. • Rayner Heppenstall • David Herbert • Gustaw Herling
Hermann Hesse • Shere Hite • Stewart Home • Abdullah Hussein
King Hussein of Jordan • Ruth Inglis • Grace Ingoldby • Yasushi Inoue
Hans Henny Jahnn • Karl Jaspers • Takeshi Kaiko • Jaan Kaplinski • Anna Kavan
Yasunuri Kawabata • Nikos Kazantzakis • Orhan Kemal • Christer Kihlman
James Kirkup • Paul Klee • James Laughlin • Patricia Laurent • Violette Leduc
Vernon Lee • József Lengyel • Robert Liddell • Francisco García Lorca
Moura Lympany • Dacia Maraini • Marcel Marceau • André Maurois • Henri Michaux
Henry Miller • Miranda Miller • Marga Minco • Yukio Mishima • Quim Monzó
Margaret Morris • Angus Wolfe Murray • Atle Næss • Gérard de Nerval • Anaïs Nin
Yoko Ono • Uri Orlev • Wendy Owen • Arto Paasilinna • Marco Pallis • Oscar Parland
Boris Pasternak • Cesare Pavese • Milorad Pavic • Octavio Paz • Mervyn Peake
Carlos Pedretti • Dame Margery Perham • Graciliano Ramos • Jeremy Reed
Rodrigo Rey Rosa • Joseph Roth • Ken Russell • Marquis de Sade • Cora Sandel
George Santayana • May Sarton • Jean-Paul Sartre • Ferdinand de Saussure
Gerald Scarfe • Albert Schweitzer • George Bernard Shaw • Isaac Bashevis Singer
Patwant Singh • Edith Sitwell • Suzanne St Albans • Stevie Smith • C.P. Snow
Bengt Söderbergh • Vladimir Soloukhin • Natsume Soseki • Muriel Spark
Gertrude Stein • Bram Stoker • August Strindberg • Lee Seung-U
Rabindranath Tagore • Tambimuttu • Elisabeth Russell Taylor • Anne Tibble
Roland Topor • Miloš Urban • Anne Valery • Peter Vansittart • José J. Veiga
Tarjei Vesaas • Noel Virtue • Max Weber • Edith Wharton • William Carlos Williams
Phyllis Willmott • G. Peter Winnington • Monique Wittig • A.B. Yehoshua
Marguerite Young • Fakhar Zaman • Alexander Zinoviev • Emile Zola